Cruelties

ALSO BY LISE BISSONNETTE

Following the Summer

Affairs of Art

Cruelties

Stories

LISE BISSONNETTE

Translated by Sheila Fischman

Published in 1998 by
House of Anansi Press Limited
34 Lesmill Road, Toronto, ON
Canada M3B 2T6
Tel. (416) 445-3333
Fax (416) 445-5967
E-mail: Customer.Service@ccmailgw.genpub.com

02 01 00 99 98   1 2 3 4 5

CANADIAN CATALOGUING IN PUBLICATION DATA

Bissonnette, Lise
[Quittes et doubles. English]
Cruelties
Translation of: Quittes et doubles.
ISBN 0-88784-630-0

I. Title. II. Title: Quittes et doubles.

PS8553.I877288Q5713 1998   C843'.54   C98-931892-3
PQ3919.2.B52Q5713 1998

Cover: Angel Guerra
Typesetting: ECW Type & Art, Oakville
Printed and bound in Canada

*House of Anansi Press gratefully acknowledges the
Canada Council for the Arts and the Ontario Arts Council
for their support of our publishing program.*

for Godefroy-M. Cardinal

CONTENTS

THE SLAIN WOMEN

He read the Bible on the bellies of girls
then poured his concrete there
The city acclaimed the beauty of his towers
and the genius of the man with the cranes
Now in this harsh time the walls are cracking
and no runaway can hear
the slain women as they stir

Take the central characters in European or American or Canadian novels that turn up in these parts, then add our own, and I defy you to find anything like the one I'm about to bring into being.

Because he's of no interest.

It would never occur to a writer to give the leading role to a building contractor by the name of Jean-René Salvail, who was born in Alma to an engineer father who worked for a big aluminum company, and a part-time real estate broker mother. He has two sisters, about whom we'll hear nothing more because they will marry and be relatively happy, one to the owner of a Burger King franchise in a Montreal suburb, the other to a middle-rank public servant with the environment department. They both graduated from nursing science and are capable of being self-sufficient in the event of the divorces that will likely occur in ten years or so, but we'll learn nothing about them.

At the junior college, where he's studying science and getting more or less passing grades, Jean-René is successively interested in various things, traces of which can be seen in his bedroom with its natural pine furniture featuring a TV set fitted into the armoire: Saharan insects, video games, Robert Charlebois, weight-lifting, Pink Floyd.

Here, let me add a qualification about something. We don't yet know if it will have any repercussions. Jean-René Salvail gets perfectly tolerable grades in French and he speaks it correctly, thanks to the vigilance of his mother, who knows how important it is to express yourself clearly now at the dawn of the information revolution. If you were to root around in his dresser drawers or under the pieces of a Meccano set he never discarded, you might even find a book that is undoubtedly unknown to you but which brought a glimmer of light into his life one summer evening. *Bleeding Bread* is a solemn, impassioned, outrageous slim volume of verse by Jean-Gauguet Larouche, a local poet and sculptor who acquired a certain national notoriety during the late sixties before he categorically abandoned us to our mediocrity and went away to die by drops while he fished in the Rivière Noire, out back of his tarpaper shack. If Jean-René Salvail possesses a copy of that coarse collection of poems that lacerate us, when you can't even find a copy of it at the finest second-hand book dealers, it's because it was lent to him by his literature prof on the night after his final exams, which was also June 24, the feast of St. John the Baptist, which around here, as everyone knows, is an occasion for serious drinking.

That night, the cold had prompted not so much lust in the moonlight as a walk home with the prof, shivering, to the peaceful apartment where she lived alone, which for Jean-René amounted to the same thing. There's nothing unusual about an eighteen-year-old from a family of freethinkers losing his virginity quite uneventfully to a lonely thirty-year-old prof in the equivalent of a village. But at thirty, you need to make up a reason for welcoming between your sheets the equivalent of the first man to turn up, and Jeannine Lahaie had thought that she'd gone beyond mere rutting by deflowering his brain as well, if not his heart. She had read some lines from *Bleeding Bread* while he was still groping between her thighs after two coital acts that were rather good considering that they were his first. The ghost of Gauguet, a distant cousin of hers, had slipped away as dawn glided in between the shutters. The poet and sculptor loved the flesh above all else and that amorous dalliance had delighted him; Jeannine must have been dear to him, though he hadn't been interested in her as a child and had died before he could know her as a woman.

The fact remains that Jean-René Salvail, either to show that he was equal to the task or because he'd been touched by the edge of a pain that would be forever foreign to him, had borrowed the book after a shower and a coffee. And had never returned it. She hadn't wanted to see him again and it is unlikely that he'd have tried to push the relationship, being already well aware of what is unseemly or quite simply dangerous for a prof's job, as teaching positions were becoming scarce.

It's hard to say whether he sometimes re-reads *Bleeding Bread* and whether Gauguet, from his splendid place in hell, finds it of any interest to have been spirited away by so pallid an individual.

It may be that Jean-René Salvail gave some brief thought to enrolling in literature at the Université de Montréal, or so a young woman who was studying the harp at the Vincent-d'Indy music school and had met up with him to the point of sex in the apartment of a mutual friend thinks she remembers him confiding to her. Or was that a tenuous recollection she might have confused with that of another of the tall clean-cut men with brown hair who found favour with her at the time?

Instead, we find Jean-René at business school, where early on he developed an interest in real estate. Whether this was a cultural trait inherited from the French, who were firm friends of stone, or a cultural trait of the Francophone middle class, who had exchanged stuffing their savings into a sock for rental properties as they became urbanized, or a cultural trait peculiar to his mother's side of the family, he had an instinctive grasp of the profits to be drawn from building during a period of heavy inflation like the one that had started when he'd finished his MBA — which he'd landed with decent grades.

The fact that he knows how to read better than most of his colleagues may also have had a felicitous influence on his choice of career. Rather than limit himself to the class notes and textbooks that were a professorial industry, he checks out specialized publications fairly often, in particular, American ones that offer the additional advantage of putting the finishing touches to an indispensable knowledge of English. Great fortunes were built on concrete, granite, and glass, with the participation of the banks before and the tenants after, in a fusion of interests that will soon verge on epiphany. It's already the case in Toronto and Calgary, and Montreal is there for the taking.

Because his capital is slim and he has to create it first by confidence, he puts his brand new MBA at the service of a developer of suburban housing projects along Highway 40, at the eastern limit of Repentigny. In no time at all, he makes himself indispensable, to the point of demanding to be made an associate, heading the Chamber of Commerce, and marrying the daughter of the other major local contractor; it could even be that it wasn't out of self-interest, as you may think, but because of her vague resemblance to Jeannine Lahaie. Although this Martine is some kind of a geographer, we won't get to know her well enough to find out whether she finds poetry in relief.

He is solid, both physically and mentally, when the Caîsse de Dépôt helps to finance his first series of buildings in an industrial park on the outskirts of Montreal, where government laboratories are setting up. He has the pair, one son, one daughter, enrolled at private school and they're of no interest to us. In memory of a June 24 that seems to him the acme of a wild youth, he voted OUI in the referendum, while remaining silent and even nodding agreement when, on the board of a bank where he'd got himself a seat, bigger players scoff at the indescribable madness of the separatists and base their own self-assurance on the fear of the people they call ordinary, the guttural pronunciation that the French word requires creating a slight spray.

I couldn't tell you how he came to keel over, or even if he did so, despite the tragic events that eventually sprang from his actions.

There comes a time when the boy is a man of forty and more and has panoramic office windows that look out on the St. Lawrence and its bridges, with the horizon blocked by what we know is the American border, very sound behind the low-lying mountains. The decor is by Madame Arbour; he is unaware that she was part of all the revolutions and still holds those ideas. The art is by Riopelle, from the series of large print runs he created for those whose pleasure comes from recouping their cost rather than gazing at the works. The secretaries wear navy or beige suits, with polyester blouses that look like silk.

The normal sequence of events, without there necessarily being any giddiness or anxiety in Jean-René Salvail, is that he has dinner one day, because he can read and thinks he enjoys it, with a business writer passing through Montreal: Ivan Fallon, the Saatchi brothers' biographer, for instance, or Neil Lyndon, for Armand Hammer. The upshot is that only a patron of the arts is immortal, but that he must burn with some inner flame, even if he's the worst of the demons. Jean-René Salvail doesn't know that he is one himself. (This would have been the perfect time to reopen *Bleeding Bread* and finally understand that Jeannine was the only woman who had touched his soul with sex, but it's pointless to expect such introspection from a man who is constantly forging ahead.)

He's in a hurry. Illumination comes to him during a fishing trip near the Moisie River, in the drawer of the bedside table, in a motel where the delay of a chartered airplane has kept him and some buddies behind. There's nothing to read but the Bible, and only beer in the minibar. He leafs through the book. He's astonished at the number of rich men who inspired the authors of the Old Testament, at the fascination wealth and power exerted on them, and at the supporting roles held by the wretched. Above all, he understands why the wealthy absolutely have to be wicked, for God is only interested in reprimand and atonement. As for the poor, they are wise and are praised with polite remarks that you sense are an obligation of the Supremely Virtuous.

The next evening, when the outfitting company delivers girls along with the smoked salmon, he doesn't need to get drunk to be ready for action. As he pulls on his condom or empties himself onto the navel of a fairly pretty woman with big hair, he thinks he's entitled and that he resembles no one else.

Neither lust nor plunder will attain great summits in him, as far as I know. He pays better than most of the consultants who inflate the rental prospects on towers like the ones he erects in the downtown core, which his vision is in fact helping to expand as far as some formerly disadvantaged neighbourhoods. Before the board of Laval's most luxurious golf club, he recommends admitting a labour leader, whose flowered shirts clash with the linen appropriate to the green. The crane operators then agree to work overtime on building sites, where an enviable peace prevails. He provides wine for the dinners of a young municipal councillor, whose conscience is uneasy as soon as zoning regulations change. He supports lawyers whose only scruple is having none. And he sleeps, once a week, with women who are not Martine.

He is the man of the cranes. The whole city acclaims the beauty of his towers.

He is the man of the cranes. God decries the infamy of his sins.

And his female companions do not fear him, for he is the lamb of God who sweetens the copulations of the world. He asks only to be drunk before he lays his head on their vulvas, which he leaves in peace. He reads strange verses.

A man impure in the body of his flesh — will have no
    rest until he has lighted a fire.
To the impure man all bread is agreeable — he will be
    calm only when he is dead.
The man emerging from the conjugal bed — says inside
    his soul: "Who can see me?
"All around me is darkness, and the walls hide me — no
    one sees me. What have I to fear?
"The Almighty will not remember my sins." — But it is
    the eyes of man that he fears.
And he knows not that the eyes of the Lord — are
    thousands of times brighter than the sun.
That they look at all the ways of men — and penetrate
    into the most deeply hidden corners.
Before they were created, all things were known to him
    — and just as much after they were created.
That man will be punished in the public square — and
    where he least expected it, he will be caught.

Young women follow one another and they resemble one another or they don't, other empty bodies suck them in, it makes no difference to him, he is only interested in the Almighty and in those whom He created in His image. He is reading Chapter 23 of the Book of the Ecclesiastic, which threatens him more directly, when his reading is interrupted. He is required in the evening, nearly every evening, to be at the office, where his acolytes are bustling about, worried about a situation that seems to be turning difficult.

As for the rest, newspapers and magazines have repeated it ad nauseam. The analysts who used to celebrate the great real estate fortunes now agree to deplore them as being built on sand, inveighing against the improvident, accusing the banks of complacency and the tax experts of cunning, discovering complicity on the part of public financing companies, insisting that heads must roll. Cameras sweep the empty premises, the unfinished towers, the paralyzed building sites. Freelancers who used to churn out dazzling profiles of Jean-René Salvail and his like now sell equally dazzling retrospectives of the errors of their ways and harsh descriptions of their falls. Vice-presidents of finance companies lose their jobs, deputy ministers are demoted. The cranes of what was once Salvail Inc. are sold off south of the American border. Martine keeps, in her own name, some suitcases in a safe place near Nassau, where she is resting with the children while her husband looks for a paid position. He'll find one, one that doesn't exploit his abilities to the fullest and will leave him in a certain stupor till he retires. Small suppliers declare bankruptcy and some commit suicide. The jobless are condemned to remain so. Hack writers cling to their only metaphor, the bursting bubble, which makes for a lot of bubbles whose shreds they will examine rather lazily, unaware that what they're chronicling is the end of a world.

And that is what you see, with your eyes that are not a thousand times brighter than the sun.

But it is otherwise in the bubble of the just, the one that's rising up into the empyrean.

The man's sperm gushed into the mouths of girls. They closed their eyes as they swallowed. They drank the ass's milk they'd read about in a Bible story. They kissed their rough wedding veils. They licked the honey they would have churned with their children. The male's ejaculate grated against their esophagi. It thickened in their stomachs. It hardened in their intestines. The girls died, clenched around their concrete bellies. There he laid his head upon his deathless work and, through the Book, he praised the wisdom of beautiful women.

In the city which he loved likewise, there did he bid me rest (Book of the Ecclesiastic, Chapter 24, Verse 11).

There were rose-coloured towers, dove-coloured towers, coal-coloured towers, almond-coloured towers, gay shrouds in which he buried his lovers. They were the cornerstone, the foundation of his glory. In the city's entrails it would come about that they heard one another bemoaning their lives that had not come to pass, which would have been more upright than the towers. One night, they recognized each other and talked about how insignificant the man was. They moved. And saw that they could move. It was the beginning of winter, the water was freezing in the fissures of hastily erected structures, the walls cracked, collapsed on the powerful, and tumbled onto the passersby, their debtors. Only the humble and the meek of heart, who did not think of running away and whose low houses had avoided ruin, celebrated with the slain women.

THE CALLIOPE

The musician shuts himself away with his calliope
Breathes its fumes, muffles its reason
To make it sing
He burned double basses, oboes, and clarinets
He'd come to the viols when the orchestra fell silent
The calliope has played off-key
the arpeggio of the dying

Music, my family has music in its blood. My grandmother, Mary Shaw, who was born in Brooklyn to an Irish family that's known to have produced violinists from one generation to the next, was a dresser at the Metropolitan Opera, no less, even though my mother, who hated her for giving birth to the drunk who would become her husband, claims that she was actually a washerwoman. What is certain is that for a long time Mary Shaw had fingered both coarse cotton undergarments and ribbons of chiffon and that she was an expert on the secretions, both intimate and public, of the singers, who in her day were very heavy and sweated copiously.

And she knew that it was at the Met that my own destiny was set. In 1889, as all the books on the opera have noted, the Metropolitan had finally presented *Der Fliegende Holländer*, forty-six years after its première at the Hofoper in Dresden and six years after Richard Wagner's death. The role of Senta, say the books, was sung by Sophie Wiesner. History has preserved only the German version of that first night at the Met, while it was followed, according to the wishes of Maestro Anton Seidl, by an Italian version featuring Emma Albani. One week before the curtain rose on *Il Vascello Fantasma*, as *L'Olandese volante* was then called, the French-Canadian soprano, who was approaching the downward slope of her mature years and could have been Senta's mother, was stricken with a gastroenteritis the effects of which Mary was required to eliminate between rehearsals. They struck up a friendship through that strange gift women have for taking the greatest interest in the slightest illness, and Mary was invited to accompany Emma during a brief visit with the Lajeunesse family in Montreal, whom the singer saw less and less frequently since her European triumphs.

I think Mary was in love with Emma. By dint of handling her petticoats, some of them lovely and lacy, she often found herself dreaming about the plump buttocks and the firm breasts in shades of pink that were far removed from the yellowing abdomen of her husband, whose woolen underwear was constantly turning grey in spite of all her care. Instinctively, she had refused to give him more than the one son, Sean, who was about to turn ten, who was lanky, and who was displaying some aptitude for the piano. She was determined that he would have a musical destiny; even if he should also become a dresser at the Met and turn out to love men, it would be all the same to her, as long as he was less vulgar than his progenitor.

Before leaving Mary behind and boarding a steamship for London and Covent Garden, where her star would soon decline, the diva gave her a peculiar present. In a pawnshop window on Craig Street next to a furrier's shop, where Mary could caress Emma through the intermediary of a beaver coat without its showing, they spied what appeared to be a brightly coloured barrel organ engraved with what, aside from a few details, was very like the set for the Met's production of the *Vaisseau fantôme*. With its sails rent by the storm but its masts intact, the unfortunate Vanderdecken's vast ship, as presented by the Met, its dimensions incompatible with the cliffs it brushed past, was sailing off forever in the setting sun; the frail silhouette of Senta cast its final shadow beneath a coral moon before it plunged into the ocean; the rocks were washed by the tears of inhuman loves. It was a mere calendar image and you could tell that the person in New York who'd drawn it had plagiarized some cheap colour print. Emma gave Mary the object for her son, as a token of gratitude for services rendered and in the hope that the young man would find in it, as they had, some reinforcement of his destiny.

The instrument was a calliope, manufactured in America. My father never became a dresser at the Met but he did take an interest in that ersatz organ, in perfect condition with its steam-powered mechanism. He dismantled it, cleaned it, oiled it, reassembled it, varnished it until he fell in love with the profile of Senta, which he appropriated for himself by transposing for the calliope Wagner's score, which was said to be his first brilliant and truly symphonic composition. Starting from the principle that the organ is an orchestra in itself, Sean made of the *Vaisseau* leitmotif an arrangement that was quite faithful and all the more remarkable because he rendered the opera in a single act, following a wish of the composer's that was granted only in 1901 in Bayreuth, and of which my father was surely unaware.

But he had talent and he found a certain favour in the era of the silent movies. He took his calliope with him to various orchestra pits and he punctuated the dramas on screen with the strains of the thwarted loves of Senta and the Dutchman, or of stormy nights on the Norwegian coast. It produced a fine effect that took him from city to city, including Montreal, where he met my mother and began to drink after he'd married her. This was logical for she was nasty and jealous of the girls whose dances he accompanied when he had to reinvent himself after the talkies arrived, in the light orchestra that was highly regarded by nightclubs. The success of these orchestras was due to their unusual instruments, and none was more unusual than the calliope as it emitted its sensual fumes and moaned under the fingers of a wine-soaked musician.

The Calliope 17

It's possible that my mother also had music in her blood, in spite of appearances and the blank silence she maintained in the series of hovels we lived in from 1915 until the end of World War II.

According to Mary Shaw, who gave back as much hostility as she'd got, the little bird who'd consented to be raped in the orchestra pit after the final performance of *Tess in the Land of Storms* — though it was winter, she was muffled in heavy clothing, and the torchères in the auditorium were still lit — had used the charms of the calliope and its Nordic storms as her pretext for approaching a boy who was ripe in years and would have been still a virgin had not some friends of his mother's taken it into their heads to rid him of his innocence before their menopause. Be that as it may, my parents attributed to one another the sin that I can't imagine them committing and they grated against one another from my beginning until their end. It was only because of an agreement between Irish Catholics from Brooklyn and French-Canadian Catholics from Montreal that I wasn't born in a hospital for unwed mothers; our household was a very chilly one. But had it not been for the torpor and suppressed rage that reigned there, I would never have paid any attention to my father's ramblings on the art of Richard Wagner, whose unhealthy and harmonious sounds I'd grasped before I'd even heard a note, the sound of the calliope being forbidden under our roof.

I have written a lot about Richard Wagner; that is, I've copied articles about him and his work from reference books, paying particular attention obviously to *Der Fliegende Holländer*, an opera totally unknown in Montreal, but I am committing an anachronism by pointing it out because as a teenager I didn't know what an opera was. Or spinsters. Or a sailing ship. Or a Dutchman. Or the sea. Upon my brain, which was as blank as the bleakness of my mother's silence, the everlasting love of Senta and the sailor were imprinted without an image. It stemmed from a single black line between two souls whom the catechism told me were pure spirits, which made their embrace a sin. Thus did they cry with a desire I took for remorse. Thus did they create, without a sound, music. I could have been born deaf, I wouldn't have heard the difference. It's a question of privilege: in my opinion I am freer than you are, I've never turned my music into cinema, even after I finally got to know the opera, the stupid opera.

When the clubs decided the calliope was too large and bulky and my father, too big a drunk, he stayed home for a few days and then died of the cirrhosis my mother'd been hoping for. Beforehand, we chatted a little, very little because he spoke English, which I hadn't really mastered. *You must swear that you won't destroy my calliope. It's the greatest instrument ever invented for playing Wagner, howling and roaring as we should, Son, as we should.* Thanks to my hunch about the black line between two souls, at least I understood the meaning of the oath. I stopped my mother from destroying the calliope she'd have put out with the trash, along with the memory of Emma and of Mary, both of whom died in their eightieth year without ever seeing the other again. Which in her eyes proved that the present, found in a pawnshop on Craig Street, was as mediocre as their supposed friendship, to which her mother-in-law had clung so tightly during a life that was more mediocre still.

I was thirty years old, I was a clerk in the accounting department of a leather goods wholesaler, I escaped with the calliope to a rooming house on Sainte-Famille Street, where I undoubtedly crossed paths with the artists you are beginning to venerate now, sculptors and poets, whereas I was the only one who translated your souls, those that were genuine, fearful, and evanescent as your wills.

I, too, had avoided the war but at least I had the excuse of being in frail health. I had mastered the calliope, recreated note by note my father's phantom ship. I'd injected it with my mother's anger and brought back to life the purest wailing that had been given it since the original sin. A young girl, very fair and very angelic, with myopic eyes that would have found certain naked skins sublime, knocked at my door and begged me to flow into her belly. I refused. I drank only water, I ate only raw things; in that way I could afford to burn the most precious woods to produce steam for my calliope. And therein lay the secret Sean had touched upon.

Which I would possess.

It took years. Montreal was a village deep in the steppes for anyone who wanted more than the most pedestrian music. From New York I ordered the score for *The Flying Dutchman*. I waited several months for it, during which time I learned to read orchestral compositions from an old European musicologist mocked by the generations who already preferred Stravinsky to Wagner, whose audience wouldn't have filled half a hall. I made a stab at German to study the original versions of books that decode the styles and craftsmanship of the German organs, which seemed to me the only ones that could imitate and render all the instruments the Wagnerian opus required. You will find, notably, in the little suitcase that I'm leaving to my landlady what for me was the wonder of the treatise by H. Klotz, *Über der Orgelkunst, der Gotik, der Renaissance und des Barocks* (Kassel, 1934), which, along with the briefer *Das Portativ* by H. Hickmann (Kassel, 1930), enabled me to give to a scale-model instrument the subtleties of the five-keyboard organ from the Hauptkirche in Hamburg, which was built at the end of the seventeenth century.

It's true that my threadbare suit and my badly cut greying hair made me look like some poor wretch when I finally asked an overworked secretary for an appointment with the maestro, whom I rather admired for his pioneering work hereabouts, and who I believed would be the first to go into ecstasies over my discovery. At most I succeeded, after a siege of several days in an office as dusty as the certainties of those people, in getting a young pianist who had in the past played the organ in the seminary to come out of pity to see and hear my oddity.

The morning was as white and pure as a Christmas, my coals were ebony, my keys were dawn and dusk, my leitmotifs belonged to eternity. He was jealous, the lad, I sensed the ochre line from his soul to my own during the final measures — *you know nothing, my fate is unknown to you* — before he rushed out, leaving behind the leather gloves that protected his slender, ridiculous hands from mine, which were veined, gnarled, heavy from all the impossible and, henceforth, successful harmonies. Hands of a convict he might have feared, on whom he took such fine revenge the following week, in his elegant handwriting.

You will also find on pure vellum paper the note he addressed to me. *I do not know, Sir, if the instrument that you alone in this city have mastered or possessed, your calliope, is masculine or feminine in gender, as the term does not appear in any dictionary of the French language. Our research indicates that a Massachusetts inventor, whom we French Canadians would call a "patenteux," obtained a patent for that singing mechanism in 1855 but its use became widespread only after 1880, without ever going much beyond the limits of New England. To our knowledge this calliope belongs to the category of circus or fairground instrument, where it would be appreciated on account of its strong tonality that was capable of attracting crowds from far away. Having no term of comparison, I would be unable to evaluate the sound you draw from it, but I do recognize that it is astonishingly versatile and I have so indicated to the maestro. He begs me to inform you however that it would not be possible for him to grant your wish to present at least a concert version of* Der Fliegende Holländer. *On the one hand, he would fear that the copious fumes given off by your calliope might harm the string instruments, which are exceptionally fragile. And on the other hand, he believes that Montreal audiences would be rather unreceptive to the lesser-known works of Herr Wagner in general and to that one in particular, whose libretto is of a dubious moral fibre and far too vividly romantic. As you will see, I regret my inability to assist you in any way other than by suggesting that you offer your services instead, before the summer now impending, to some place of popular entertainment such as Sommer Park, where it might be interesting to accustom the people to a melodic line less insignificant than that which has satisfied street performers for far too long. We for our part would be most appreciative.*

Nowhere in the records of your metropolis of Nordic insignificance will you find this story, the only explanation for the mysterious cancellations of concerts that occurred in April 1952, a month before the end of the season said by the press to have been cut short because the maestro was indisposed.

They'll swallow anything, the newspapers and their critics, those bystanders on the fringes of life. The truth is that for days, or rather nights, my now dying calliope began to demand increasingly precious woods. To please her, I stole the double basses, then the clarinets, and then the oboes. She tasted a great deal of the viols, the theft of which finally put the police on red alert. Thanks to their stirring convolutions, I was almost able to give her a human voice — the voice of Senta rising up in your streets while the orchestra fell silent.

You paid it no attention. For a long time you'd been dashing off to watch colour flicks in malodorous movie theatres, from which the orchestra pits had disappeared. I no longer went out. In lilac time I had left only embers. On a perfect evening, my calliope played off-key.

You, who will never rise above your noise, don't try to tell me I could have survived.

THE CHAINS

She kissed her vanity
she who danced in red
with chains at the ankles
A free man began to caress the chains
and was consumed there before dawn

She walks into the hunchbacked professor's house, which smells of overcooked cabbage and old man. He lives on an English street, in a house with a verandah and windows lined with plastic because it's winter and drafts mustn't come in, his bones ache. He takes her coat and shakes it, though it isn't snowing, as if to shed the night that is falling, but not into his home, which is bright with its halogen lights. He shows her into the sitting room, the tea has already brewed, he offers to perk it up with mint-flavoured alcohol, she accepts, she has come here to get him on her side.

At school, she usually sees him in profile, a bald head that is like a hook above the white smock that hangs, at an angle because of the hump, over lean trousers. Face on, in the foam-cushioned chair where his back disappears, he's as erect as the colonel he would have liked to be, this man who bellows orders in the studio. This evening, he speaks more softly but it's his eyes that crackle. They are the colour of nails.

Nothing can be heard save footsteps in the nearby kitchen, which must have a wood floor, artists always being fond of wood but usually of music as well. His own passion it would appear is for books; he's written some that have disappeared from sight — but that's just art school gossip. She believes she is the first to enter here and if there were tragedies in the past, now there is only the smell of cabbage soup. Its scent hangs heavily on the walls where Molinaris clash with Tousignants from the right period. She would have expected him to collect drawings, he being the only one who still knows how to teach it.

"You see," he tells her, "I'm certain that you're ver[y] talented but also that you have nothing to say." Sinc[e] she requested this interview as a student with better-than[-]average grades who wants to strengthen her position, sh[e] does not flinch at the assault, she was expecting it, that's hi[s] style. There's a chill all the same, between her bare knee[s] and along her thighs, her lycra skirt pulls up when sh[e] sits down. She tugs on the hem, for no reason or to indi[-]cate submission. It's not a question of rebelling. "I'm n[ot] mature, I'm well aware of that, but actually I'd like to g[o] further, to improve myself." She senses an opening, th[e] word "improve" will unlock it in this man who's obsesse[d] with accomplishment and despised by his younger col[-]leagues. In his habit of addressing others by their surname[,] a practice unique to him, she has foreseen a gold mine: th[e] manners she could inherit, the ties to the ancient academies[,] the supports that would be hers on the day when classica[l] drawing dislodges formless expressionisms, it will come[,] it always does — the renewal of art along the old trails[.] But he is creaking, his reaction confirms that she is empty[,] perfection is a matter of form, which she has alread[y] achieved. He repeats this, she is incapable of having any[-] thing to say.

The tea is too green, the mint-flavoured alcohol doesn'[t] sweeten it. She's about to get annoyed, to ask him wh[y] he has summoned her, at an hour when men are finishin[g] their day's work and looking for an ass to put their han[d] on, she'd have that at least to tell this man who is a fan[-] atic about studies of nudes. She's restraining herself. She'[ll] explode later on, when he asks her to pose for him, al[l] alone in this house, it's inevitable, the mint alcohol mus[t] be the trick of an aged lady's man, he's wearing a velve[t] jacket, he hides his crumpled neck with a Mao collar, sh[e] will tell him he smells of cabbage and she'll slam the door.

The hunchback's eyes don't give way. He speaks now with no interstices. For twenty-eight years he has been teaching drawing, which he'd learned from books during a month in hospital after an accident that left him rich, from the compensation, but deformed, insignificant, and scrawny, and made him go unnoticed among the magnificent youth of the sixties. He had moved to Paris and attended the École des beaux-arts on rue Bonaparte when the France of future unwashed artists was stammering its first words of English so as to give titles in the style of New York, while the Québécois Quasimodo wore himself out in every collection of drawings in every museum, in search of the perfect line. He'd found thousands, amid a tension that drained him, that gave him migraines severe enough to make him want to throw himself into the Seine. They didn't leave him until he unearthed a red chalk drawing in which the line came alive; even architects could do it, by colouring their preliminary drawings. Purple, bordeaux, ochre, carmine, amaranth, rose, amber: there's nothing like blood to give meaning.

He wants to know if she has any in her fingers, her hand, her eye, she whose drawing of a beautiful young man viewed from the rear, slathered with cream pastel, had given him a little respite one evening when he was doing his corrections. It must have been an accident but you never know. He even came up with the idea of putting her to the proof, of offering her his studio in which to produce a drawing in red chalk —on the condition that it be a self-portrait. She would have to look at herself, to plunge into the void that he suspects is there. And if she should find something, in spite of the white that he sees now floating between them, he would have been wrong. He wants it to be so to free him of those migraines, which are like steel now.

She murmurs consent, the privilege goes well beyond the hopes she had when she first came here, she has no studio but the ones at the school and she is sure of her ability, in such a place and with such a master. He helps her on with her coat without touching her, it is she who forces the contact by extending her hand, which she realizes is warm. In the bus she boards at the corner of Greene and Sherbrooke, she sees that most of the people are misshapen; indeed, it's better that she make her own portrait, she is rather well-shaped and she knows every line of her face, it takes her half an hour every morning to colour it indiscernibly. She goes home to her mother's, a divorced intellectual with a fine library of art books, surely she has one about self-portraits.

To enter the studio one must pass through a sort of tunnel on the mezzanine level, then go up towards an immense skylight that abuts an exterior wall of the house but is insulated like a greenhouse. This morning, the snow is gliding across the glass roof with its copper joints the colour of the Paris rooftops she has seen in books. The light builds up around the tables as if it is pouring in from the winter garden, it races across the travertine floor, is multiplied in the display cabinets that protect an infinite number of tubes, crayons, measures, rags. And breaks like a wave on the mirror he has set up in the sole free space, a cheval glass that could have come from Ikea, with its plain pale frame. Narrow and tall, it can contain nothing more than a young woman with hips that barely flare. Before he hands her the keys to the cabinets, he asks if it will do. She says yes. She sees him in profile today but without a smock. His torso is high, his legs long, he must have been a good-looking man before his accident; she thinks it's a shame but she doesn't like thinking about it. The few men she's had sex with were in good health.

Since he wanted blood red, she's gone whole hog. She is

wearing a red dress, long and straight except for a flare at
the ankles and a seam under the breasts that suggests an
Empire waist. It is sleeveless, with a round, modest neck,
cut rather low in the back because she wore it last Christmas, but she's not drawing herself from the back. The room
is filled with dry heat, flawlessly draught-proof, she'll move
easily here. She notices there's no door to the garden, he has
built himself a crystal prison, it's weird, this love of light
and this disdain for air.

Every morning, for three hours, she draws, alone.

At first, things go well. She amasses sketches of a young
woman who does not yet resemble her, line for line; she's
becoming familiar with the lines of the body reflected in the
cheval glass, is surprised to see a slightly low waist, square
shoulders, realizes that she has rarely observed from close-
up anything but her breasts and her belly, is amused by the
details. What's most complicated is finding the angle at
which to place herself in the rigid frame. She would like to
give herself some fluidity, to blur the long lines of the
profile, to retain some mystery. But he would not allow
himself to be misled by the trickery of a beginner who is
circumventing the difficulties, she must draw herself full-
face, with no shadows; in fact, there's no room for shadow
in red or pink, it turns into the most insignificant of greys.

By the fifteenth hour, she can no longer postpone tackling
the face. The outline is fine, an ordinary oval, the head
slightly raised as in a fashion photo — women have straight
necks, now and forever. She rather likes her broad forehead,
which will remain unwrinkled, like her mother's, they both
have slightly oily skin, the best protection against time as
long as you keep it scrupulously clean. But she goes back
again and again to the eyes, and the lips. The expression
she sees in the mirror isn't hers, she is certain of that, after

all, she doesn't have that heart-shaped mouth and those big, lazy brown eyes like a dog's. Seen from inside, she has always thought of her lips as smiling and sensual, her laughing eyes as chestnut brown. In fact, that's why she likes to call them chestnut, the word sounds spring-like and crunchy, for an expression that's kind and intelligent. What she sees come into view on the paper is an adorable little face, pretty like so many others. She works doggedly, gives herself airs that don't belong to her, she lies with pencil lines that become welts, soon she'll turn herself into a witch and kill that smile. As for the eyes, that's simple, she will close them, it will be a blind self-portrait, such a thing must exist, and if not, she will have invented it.

She is sweating now, though the sun is cold, the dress sticks to her belly, she should leave here rather than let her anger rise. In the empty sockets beneath the elegant and perfectly drawn eyelids, she sees the trap in which he has locked her. She is twenty years old and soon more, she knows nothing. Save for some few thousand words for naming drink, food, sex, the colour of the day, the odour of the street and the passing seasons, she knows nothing. In that man and in the pain that haunts him there are places, memories, questions that will never touch her. She is like her friends from school, children with smiles, cloned in a land that extends, neither sad nor happy, in idiotic America, healthy vegetables, scions rid of the share of horror that used to accompany intelligence in the past. At twenty, one does not make a new background for one's eyes, the task is impossible, he will have won.

All that remains is rage at the tips of red-stained fingers. It will take her an entire day to make the big full-length drawing, the final one, the red chalk drawing of a dress the colour of blood, worn by a young woman with a low waist and a vacant look, whose bare arms frame her belly as if to offer it for sale, the look dances as far as the pubis. The legs, however, are frozen beneath the silk, the ankles are gripped in the grey shadow that the bloodred chalk precludes but she must have it, for she is drawing her chains, huge charms that fall onto her pretty feet, rusty jewels joined together by a bar of steel. The key she tosses into her memory, which does not exist, and then she leaves.

The hunchback comes home late that afternoon, as usual. He knows she has finished, she has closed the mezzanine door behind her. He goes directly to the studio, he switches on all the lights, the big drawing is lying on the table, he staples it to the frame of the mirror, which disappears.

He knew it, he knew he was the girl's lover, that he had never encountered any other. The hollow head in which he could empty out his pain without danger, endlessly. The body offered full face, which he will enter directly, tearing the silky paper with his still virgin sex. The imprisoned ankles to which he thinks he alone has the key.

He looks for it in the pile of rejections that has been his life, he strokes the chains, the mark of the lock, he must turn it twice, keep her in her cage, she who has taken all the steel from his head and used it to adorn her ankles, she who has understood and who will draw their embrace forever, following orders. He presses himself to the paper, he is burning face on, there where he is still a handsome man he feels the steel melt beneath his brow.

In the morning the housekeeper who cooks the cabbage soup for him finds him stretched out cold in his studio, his head between the feet of a life-sized drawing of a woman in red. She is blind, he is hunchbacked, she is trampling him with her chains, it's as if he has hanged himself there. Death scene in red chalk. A surrealist picture.

THE VIPER

Warmed in your bosom
the viper weeps
She has drunk there milk
more poisonous than her tears
As Medusa is dying, my daughter with skin of clay,
my grief is unending
I had given her life
so her venom would carry you off

The idea came to me, the time was right, on my return from Mexico. I had called her from Mirabel, as if she were expecting me there at home, in the house where I'd settled her eight years before, a perfect little house on the road to Lac Bruyère but five minutes from the college so that I could have lunch there after my morning classes, see how her work was progressing, change the printer ribbon as necessary, regulate the heat or air-conditioning, go through the mail, agree on the errands I'd do before six so that she could write in peace all afternoon, and so that, come evening, we would have nothing more to do than admire the day's two pages that add up to a two-hundred-and-fifty-page novel every year, counting the long rest I arrange for her every summer, which is always the most beautiful, in our own yard, between the vines I've managed to make climb the back wall covered with aluminum siding and the rock that has ended up on our property, tall and bare. It protects her from any eyes but mine, she couldn't bear that, she has to be able to think in peace about the next story she'll move on to in the fall.

Her voice had its usual tone, smooth, slightly detached, but wasn't I the one who had taught her to feed her moods into her computer where they become so fertile? I was on my way home, I'd be there in eight hours, that is to say the middle of the night, if the road was clear, which she thought it was since it hadn't snowed since my departure three days earlier, for a symposium on cultural free trade in North America, during which time she had written six pages. I would read them the following day.

I could have come home by plane, an hour and a half at most counting the stop at Val-d'Or, but I need to drive across the La Vérendrye preserve, to savour every moment that takes me away from the idiotic crowd, each of the kilometres that were the miles of my inane childhood, eaten away by the desire to leave, the wrong I had done for which I would now make amends by reconstructing my memories, of black flies and blue skies, of biting ice and burnt spruce trees, where a boy grew with the strength of his country, ready to become the man she knew. I have travelled widely, with her I've come back to my roots, for she needed air and silence. She's a great writer, you know.

She didn't get up when I parked the car on our square of gravel. She's a light sleeper but it was four a.m. and normal that she wouldn't want to ruin the day ahead; I thought about it in the shower and again as I slipped in beside her. It seemed to me that her body was tepid, not warm, but that could be simply a mistaken impression, I was too tired to really sense such subtle differences. More than anything I wanted to sleep, I had a class at nine a.m.

At breakfast, which I fix myself, for I'm the only one who knows the correct proportions for the coffee, I gave her the siren from the Balderas market. I have a knack for unearthing beautiful objects. This one is amazing. According to the woman who sold it to me for eighty dollars Canadian, a pittance, it's a contemporary piece. I think so, too, because of the siren's breasts, which are large and pointed, with bright red areolas like those on hookers in European comic strips. The head is that of an Aztec with black eyes and hair, worn short and combed back smoothly — another feature of our day which I saw on the beggar women who prowl the bazaars. The body, however, is heavy with the most remote and the most enduring legends of this people I don't know well, whom I'd thought were haunted by death. Lying on the dorsal spine as if it had loomed up from a sea of gilded scales, a lizard laughs, clinging tight, held comfortably there by the creature's superb tail, which rises and falls into folds like a bloodsucker in the sun. Red as her fins and her areolas, the fringe foams as in an orgasm and it is one. For in the place where the tail curls, a black serpent, coiled in circles, its penis firm, drives its sting into some consenting, hidden flesh. And how they come, all three of them.

The belly is that of a fish, the eyes a woman's, the cry a cry of the living.

I suggested that she listen to the cry and put it into a book, she writes quite naturally about the erotic.

The idea came to me to kill her and then drive her crazy. I mean, when I was disembarking from the plane, because I had to return to my erroneous country, to my ill-chosen woman, I murdered her first of all in my head.

I proceeded that way because I'm an intellectual, my hands are too delicate to strangle or shoot without faltering and I would loathe prison where slender men like me are fucked in the ass by beefy guys caked in filth. Once she'd been eliminated, I would only have to obliterate her with acid, like the victims of Marie Davaillaud, the widow of a man named Besnard who died, free, at the age of eighty-four after leaving her body to science, which her poisonings had outsmarted, and with panache because in France books are still written about her that even make their way over here. I carefully studied her method, which was based on the presence of arsenic in every human organism — small quantities that must be gradually increased. In that way I would distill the faint madness that also occurs in small quantities in the brain of every writer, in homeopathic but increasing amounts up until the end of the spring term, so that I could hand over a madwoman to the home for lunatics who are so well forgotten at the asylum in Malartic, while I took off thanks to the one-year unpaid leave to which I'm entitled.

All I'd need when I came home from the college every day would be to find a flaw in her interpretation of ecstasy in the siren from the Balderas market. First a colour dulled by words, then an earth smell in a creature of the sea, then something improbable about the caresses exchanged by vertebrate and invertebrate species and, finally, a significant error of agreement in the sound of the simultaneous orgasm of the siren, the lizard, and the serpent. As everyone knows, it must screech across skins of clay, which requires an atonality that's difficult to translate into words.

As of early February, it would be easy. She wouldn't be up to it. I would come home later and later to find her more and more dishevelled and crazed, very softly I would refer to her genius, which would surely be restored the next day, but I'd refuse to make a commitment to her publisher for fall publication. All great writers have gone through bad periods, I would tell her, even as I picked out some dangling participles and misplaced modifiers. In mid-March, around six o'clock on some evening of horror, I would call a therapist who's buried away here in our part of the world, a foreigner with a dubious degree, who rumour has it raped nymphets, so that he'd work himself into the ground on the case of a woman he was bound to dislike, who exuded effort and fear under what was left of her beauty. The matter would then be concluded and my colleagues would be somewhat sympathetic to me in my sorrow, though they wouldn't be unhappy that it was happening to me, their spouses, in general, lacking in any charms that might be fading.

I would take with me the unfinished pages and the siren from the Balderas market. So as not to leave any traces, I would burn them at one of those roadside stops on Highway 117, where only indifferent travelling salesmen halt. The fire would chase away the season's first mosquitoes and I would read *La Frontière* before feeding it, too, to the flames. At Mont-Laurier I would pick up a hitchhiker, an illiterate with legs that went on forever. She would find something better than words with which to console me on the death of my wife.

Things turn out otherwise. I'm sorry.

It is midsummer, the stony ground is oozing with the heaviest heat that has ever swooped down on our dry land. My wife spends the day sleeping in a hammock hung in the only shady corner, her flanks are radiant under gauzy dresses like those we imagine on white women in southern Africa during imperial times. Until May, she refused to start on the legend of the siren from the Balderas market; after all, she had a novel to finish. I wasn't used to hearing her argue but I couldn't stop her, I have white hands and a low voice, I don't raise my hand or my voice. I waited, for nothing is more deadly to a poisoner than haste.

As it turned out I had no reason to worry. I could see that she was smitten with the siren, she stroked it far more often than she did me, her fingers lingered over every one of the grooves in a riot of caresses we now practise only rarely.

When we went into raptures over the last pages of her latest novel, she began sleeping during the daytime and writing at night. She refuses my presence, scribbles in a grey notebook she keeps under lock and key, says it's time to renew her style and ours, and to let herself be inspired by the summer when words breathe differently. The story would be brief and completed before September, she said. I still had no reason to worry. I'd just have to find another way to distill the faint madness; the intelligent poisoner knows how to adapt. I went about my business as if nothing were amiss, I measured out the coffee, mixed cool salads, poured white wine in the evening, bought the red-ink pens that she uses up in four or five nights.

It is twenty past three on the August day that is the feast of the Assumption, I am reading and re-reading the grey notebook that she handed me at noon. She's asleep.

It recounts the adventures of a woman with swarthy skin who turned twenty in a house with red lamps and gilt beds she had learned to keep spotless by drinking all the sperm from all the pale penises that quivered for the Indian maid. They spoke English, she read French, until she possessed all the words for hatred, including those that hide it best. Then she walked slowly to the big library with its green lamps and golden tables and smiled at a pale young man who was fantasizing about an Indian, for he was beginning to miss his northern land. They went there together, to a perfect house where he was the slave, day and night, with warmth at his back. Sometimes he took her delicately from behind, she tolerated it better than her sticky memories. She wrote acclaimed novels, he became a burden to her, she was so comfortable in the blue dusks and the golden dawns that fell and rose to the south of Lac Bruyère, when he was absent. One icy morning — though she had dreamed the night before, while talking to him on the telephone, that he had disappeared along Highway 117, which was so well laid out for death — he came back from Mexico. He had given her a wood carving that looked like papier mâché, a siren he thought was orgasmic but that she knew was merely disgusted, who was giving birth to a viper while a lizard was breaking her back. The fish-woman's story had a happy ending, fortunately, because the viper was stillborn; that was obvious to anyone who knew anything about bites and snakes, the woman was an Indian and she knew. The siren would swim happily in the coldest water, and she wouldn't have any more children.

Never had I read anything so sublime from her pen. Each word found the next one amid slowly distilled rage, from the hot sex to the dead child. Handing me the notebook, she told me she was pregnant, with my daughter, whom she will feed at her breast and who will not live long. Her venom is a work of genius, my grief is unending.

WONDERS

In wonderland
she is hairy and fat
She serves as a pillow for girls with pubes of gold
sings lullabies to them
and rubs their navels
Her vulva is filled with the venom of misapprehension
She makes Alice drink there, Alice drowns in her well

The convents were being drained of their young nuns and the older ones were doling out the separation pay. The weather was the kind you dream about, one of those acid green times when you can be sixteen years old in utter cruelty. The world behind us was finished.

In the dormitories where we were the final boarders, there was no monitor. We could talk until late at night about the chrysalises that were opening before our eyes. Sister Jean-de-l'Étoile had become a Suzanne. She was already pretty with her turned-up nose and her big dark eyes, but freed of her cornet and encountered in a park near the university she was attending, she was quite simply beautiful. History doesn't tell us if she was seeing the visual arts prof with whom she sometimes shut herself away in the studio — it was our favourite piece of gossip. Sister Saint-Luc-l'Évangéliste, who was so unhappy to be teaching us physics and who we thought was ugly, between her broad forehead and her pointed chin, had changed into a magnificent panther once she'd shed the serge and the underskirts that made her full hips heavier. We had no putative lover for her but one would come, that was guaranteed. Sister Sainte-Thérèse was the same in civilian life as in her community, the grey mouse we missed now during library hour, the intelligence that warned us against printed religiosity and introduced us to contemporary novels and essays. To get her back, we'd have been glad to link her with the chaplain who was also eyeing the door, but a blonde with a Mercedes, buxom as far as we could tell, had been coming to pick him up every weekend for a while now. Neither the Church nor mother superior who represented it on the premises could be ruthless. It was a flood.

It did not yet carry us away. The flimsy dam of boarding school held fast, cracked with permissions unthinkable yesterday. We went to the movies, even during the week, even to take in stories about adulterous love. I read the *poètes maudits*, whose names were still on the Index that lay conspicuously on a lectern in the study hall. After dinner, we'd devour chips drowned in gravy at the snack bar across the street, run by a Syrian of whom the convent was no longer suspicious. Or we'd listen, at full volume and a thousand times, to our own singer-songwriters, who promised us the sea and love and the country to go with them. Francine, who was richer than the rest of us, drove us in her first Beetle to the English park in a nearby town. In copses as clean as the ponds, we savoured freedom in the form of warm 7UP and cheese sandwiches, talking about boys as if they were ants.

It was perfect, the pain we, all of us, affected at being alone, it was serving to blur our reflections, which were all alike. It rose in coils from Josiane's cigarettes, it lingered between the lines of the diary of my boredom, it made Marie-Paule despair of having everything for herself. We were languid and firm, which is impossible but creates sadness, which was necessary at bedtime when we slept in rows, all alike, wearing pyjamas, all alike.

And that was when she arrived, in early December of the last school year of the last boarding school, the day-student who didn't resemble us. She was fat. I mean square, without a waist, carved in a single block from thighs to chin. She was hairy. I mean scattered with coarse black hairs, from forearms to temples. Fat and hairy. We only looked at her on the sly. That was worse. Wide feet in laced boots, while the rest of us swayed on stiletto heels all day long. Hands that were clean and pudgy, while we embellished ours with agates. Short, straight hair, shaved nape, a bowl cut, whereas we went from permanents to rollers.

As none of us wants to talk about it today, it's very hard for me to remember, by myself, the way she domesticated us. It must have been in choir, because Sister Marguerite-de-Jésus, the strict musician, had just given up her coif and we were left to our own devices to prepare for some Christmas concert or other, we had something of a reputation in the region. I don't remember that December except with Michèle at the piano; she revitalized us with her captivating contralto voice, she gave heart to a fragile bunch of sopranos, she knew all the songs and all the jingles she led us into when we'd finished rehearsing; it took us less than a week to adopt her. Except for Francine and Josiane, whom we accused of jealousy. And so I couldn't recognize, I who poured rivers of melancholy into my diary, the first true crack in our friendship.

I have to say, it was still an infinitesimal speck. The beginning of winter was feverish; exams mingled with the airs on the guitar Michèle played as well. After the holidays we were going to write our own songs and cut a record, she promised. We separated for ten days, joyously, she left arm-in-arm with Marie-Paule, the most beautiful of us all, who was going to stay with her because Marie-Paule's mother was expecting a baby.

Innocence is the imbecilic gaze we plunged into Marie-Paule's darkly shadowed eyes when we came back. She was more beautiful than ever, languid, the nursing sister alluded to slight anemia. There were plenty of grey and white days to make her into a shadow of herself, in spite of the care Michèle took to distract her from one weekend to the next until she went back to take the country air for a while. I was an excellent contralto, I liked all the songs, I was hundreds of kilometres away from my parents, I was the next one to be invited by Michèle.

In a few hours I learned all there was to know about sin. It takes place in a house with worn linoleum, with four rooms cluttered with Formica tables and a TV set always turned on, with the smell of beer and men in shirtsleeves. Two elderly women whisper there and fry ground meat. We shut ourselves away in Michèle's room, we write on our knees, the sin is, first of all, my pity for her wretched life. Then it is a hand running along my shoulder, after that a hand grasping my wrist, then a kiss at the corner of my mouth, then the knowing smile of the women and the man at supper time and then the terror of the night. There is a mauve alarm clock with fluorescent green hands, which works. The sin is to go to the bathroom and not take that opportunity to run away; it is to go back and let oneself be touched again and again in a place where one hardly dares to wash, and to writhe and to drink the kisses. And to give back nothing, either, she doesn't ask for that. The sin is the long bus ride to the convent through that neighbourhood of robberies and fires, where we chat about choir and homework and lessons while I'm sure that I'll never go back there and that I'll go back there, perfumed, the following Saturday.

There's no harm in that, you say today on your TV shows and in your papers. But there is, there's a great deal of harm. There are lying letters, hidden embraces, songs sung off-key. New words, faded forever.

Thus the whole winter passed, with me dreading the one who had gone before me and the one who would follow me. I don't know how many she caressed. The choir had its moments of savage grace, a gold bubble where the voices of girls met in heat, in a convent whose doors were no longer bolted.

The last one to pass there, at the edge of summer, was called Alice. She was so tiny we hadn't noticed her come up from a less advanced class. Her face was that of an ornamental doll, with long thick hair that was blond, almost red, eyelashes that curled naturally, a bland little smile. Under her uniform you could imagine the soft body, the absent breasts and the lace underwear. Dolls that talk also have reedy voices that trill. The others in the choir thought she was pathetic, but since we hardly heard her and since Michèle insisted on her being there, she was part of the year-end trip to Quebec City, thirty dollars, everything included: youth hostel, chartered bus, the Plains of Abraham and the church of Notre-Dame-des-Victoires.

We travelled at night, to save money, leaving before dawn and returning at dusk, windows open onto sizzling hot roads, those who were awake in the front, the sleepers in the back. Alice was dozing on Michèle's shoulder, then she fell asleep on her lap, then she was buried in her arms. The rumour ran through our songs, the stops in leatherette restaurants where we gulped brown-water coffee let us talk about it nearly aloud. Little laughs, looks that were know-ing or dismayed. In a few hours there were half a dozen of us who had repudiated Michèle and our nights with her. We had joined the camp of Josiane and Francine, who were modest in victory. They pretended to believe female fond-ling was as foreign to us as to them, as convinced of their perversity, a word we did not yet possess but that was prowling around our whispered denunciations. Poor Alice, poor fly caught in a spider's web, poor doll only recently shattered. We wouldn't see that, fortunately; the next year we would be in classes where there were boys.

There were boys before, though, all summer long. Scattered to our various countrysides, we wrote each other letters filled with sighs and innuendo, the beginnings of the laughing confidences that would follow, that would tell of the first time, whether he'd been too slow or too fast, whether he'd said romantic things, whether touching a penis was arousing, and whether the shudder was really and truly an orgasm. We thought with pity about the pale bodies of our mothers, our own were pink and moist and we'd never make love in the dark. If we knew how to undress and to offer ourselves without shame, with the necessary hunger, it was not because of Michèle; we didn't think about her any more, she did not exist. It was because we were bright, liberated by our own means. All of us had taken back our senses, they were new and beautiful.

Twelve years later, I won't talk about it to anyone, I saw Michèle again at a pedestrian mall in the English town where I've been working for a while now. I couldn't avoid her, she came straight towards me pushing a wheelchair in which the shadow of a young woman was asleep, her mouth open, drool on her chin, her complexion waxy, her hair a dirty blond. It was Alice. The day was mild, we had a 7UP on the terrace of Sharry's, during the drawn-out noon hour of civil servants. Alice didn't wake up. She said so little about her, Michèle did, but I knew. That summer, the doll was no more afraid of the light than we were but she was holding the hand of a girl, she was drinking the juice of a woman in the bushes and kissing her in movie theatres. Alice's mother, a hussy with ringlets, her father, curt and principled, had hurled insults at her. They were pigs, passersby had agreed; a school principal had made her lose her teacher's licence in September, through an anonymous denunciation. For a few months Alice had been shattered, her mind was fragile, then one night she threw herself into the water, into one of this town's deep ponds. Now what was left was the rag that Michèle cradled, now and forever.

I may have said more than Michèle did. I held forth on the Puritanism of these English places, on the laws that are changing and the prejudices that remain, on the ravages of ignorance, on unfit parents. The hour passed between us, the sweep of green hands on a mauve clock in an elsewhere I've never visited. I took Alice's hand, I was reassuring; everyone is entitled to live freely, I assured Michèle of my friendship, offered her my assistance, just in case, knowing she didn't need it, she's strong. She wiped Alice's chin. She was about to leave. I wonder if one can call love the spark that flashed in her eyes, splendid steel in a still graceless face. Back then, it seems to me, she only had little flings.

Never mind, I don't really know how to say it, I wouldn't want you to think I'm blaming them, but. . . .

WINGS

Her master gives her wings
The first one is torn in August
the last in October
She brushed against the back of a man with a sail
towards the end
"May the lovely lady drink all the water
and give flesh to the water weeds," said he to no one
I myself only listen to boys
and I love a fire-eater

When the plane touched down in Denver, Hélène Pasquinel gave thanks to Victor-Lévy Beaulieu. While reading a brief essay entitled "Quebeckers in Colorado," reprinted from the 8 July 1978 issue of *Le Devoir* in his collection entitled *Between Sainthood and Terrorism* (VLB éditeur, 1984), she'd encountered the hero of James Michener's novel, *Colorado Saga*, also named Pasquinel, who came from Quebec. He was the first white man to explore the southern continuation of the Rockies, mostly in search of beaver pelts, animals she had not known were economically important in the United States three hundred years ago.

Such is life for a historian, driven from one reference to another but rarely guided by introspection. If Hélène had been sensitive to the coincidence of the names, she who was indifferent to her own genealogy, it was perhaps because of a mild fatigue, a weakness she'd let herself slide into this spring when she was completing her vast study of the influence of women on political ideologies in Quebec, from the suffragette movement to the present. Not that one finds many reflections on the matter in Victor-Lévy Beaulieu but someone had told her about another essay in the same volume, "Manifesto for a New Novel," in which he seemed to ascribe to the growing presence of women writers certain problems with the birth of the Quebec novel. "If Quebec women write more than the men," he had wondered in a hitherto unpublished 1965 essay, "is it because our social structures allow women more time to pursue an activity that allows them to kill that time?" Hard to believe that VLB was still asking that same sexist question thirty years later, but it seemed to Hélène that the notion of killing time was a muted evocation of the murder of the literature of anger specific to men, whose advent the writer longed for.

There was a parallel with Hélène's work, the results of which were somewhat frightening. The more women had been involved with political parties since mid-century the more their founding ideologies had been watered down It seemed that the sovereignist movement had been the one most affected by this erosion, though no irrefutable relationship of cause and effect can be established, and the independentist parties have always had male leaders Hélène had envied Victor-Lévy Beaulieu his relationship with history, made up of brilliant hunches and the freedom to express them. She'd read the whole book and let herself be carried away to Colorado. Now, in this huge sparkling airport, she just had to locate the connecting flight to Aspen.

And so in an F-28 above a black storm over the Rockies began the most wonderful week in the life of Hélène Pasquinel, who had signed up for one of the Aspen Institute's famous summer cultural seminars. She was filled with happiness at the prospect of being a student again. During the two flights, she had boned up on a book by the keynote speaker, Professor James Carbonneau, *The New Tribes of North America*, a thesis about crossbreeding as a social advantage at the dawn of the twenty-first century. An anthropologist at Berkeley, Carbonneau had rediscovered his own Québécois origin, which he had to deal with however in English, his only language. Hélène was looking forward to talking with him about Pasquinel and others like him.

Aspen was sunny, blazing hot, and strewn with trees broken by a snowstorm the day before. Pretty blonde women were assessing the damages along with the workers, the streets had been ploughed, and rosy children were at large. The receptionist at the institute's residence told Hélène, who already knew it, that Aspen's climate was subject to sudden extreme changes and that she shouldn't forget to take along the woollen blanket she'd find in her room when she went to the evening concert in the big tent. At four o'clock, Hélène was sipping iced tea on the terrace of one of the chic western-style restaurants in downtown Aspen as she gazed at the permanent snow in the distance and thought that she wouldn't like to be three hundred years younger. In their faded jeans and freshly washed T-shirts, the young waiters were themselves delicious, they had that mixture of keenness and detachment that is the sign of a potential artist. A good-looking birdbrain in a shop next door sold her a sundress with straps that crossed low down on the back, its transparency and lilac colour as extravagant as its price.

It turned cooler at precisely eight o'clock and she was wearing heavy socks when she got bored in the big tent, listening to the second-rate Aspen Symphony Orchestra perform Mozart far too cautiously. She walked home with a lady in a fuchsia parka, a retired Florida high-school teacher and Aspen regular, who advised her to be more wary of the sun than of the cold. With windows wide open, she slept under a heavy duvet the purest sleep a woman of thirty-five can experience.

And so it went for her relationship with James Carbonneau, whose seminar had attracted only ten registered students, eight of them members of a cross-cultural association that had formed via the Internet and had no need of him to get along, a Finnish socialist who was seeking an intellectual framework to combat his government's unreceptiveness to immigration, and Hélène Pasquinel, a Montreal historian who wanted to rediscover the pleasure of taking notes "Call me James," he'd said. He was quite good-looking, a tall, grey-haired, only slightly heavy sixty-something with the regular features peculiar to American athletes, an affable face tempered by eyes at once sea green and dark — an agreeable source of nervousness.

Though light, the discipline at Aspen was followed to the letter. The group met only in the morning, then scattered in the afternoon into individual meditations, yoga classes, or excursions to visit ecological discoveries at the foot of the mountains. Hélène had the impression that James was talking about her own life, though Pasquinel, she was now convinced, had never existed. Even in the shadowy enclosure where the seminar was held, she was slowly acquiring a tan. And she thought she was doing it from inside, under the sun of the words though they were in English. Crossbreeding is a personal destiny, he said, a way of being that allows one to assume and to withstand the gaze one has long brought to bear on what seemed to be a state of degeneration. The hybrid then is lucid and less and less vulnerable to domination. Through his tangled roots he is also polymorphous and he emerges the winner, the hybridization of thought being the condition today for intellectual survival.

Resistance. Audacity. At the fifth lecture, when James simply summed up what he had taught that week, Hélène wondered for a moment if he wasn't falling into American triviality. "The hybrid has wings," he had said. All things considered, she could feel them. She was Pasquinel, she now had the golden skin of a fraction of a mulatto who could have been knocked up in the local heather by a runner come in from the cold, she was ready to make a child with the man she had intermittent sex with, and to publish an incendiary thesis.

On the last evening, James left a note at the residence inviting her to dinner, ceremonious as an abbot from whom she was, nonetheless, expecting advances. Advances there were, it was so cold in the enclosure where they'd gone to sit around midnight, comparing their lives, and soon their tongues touched. But she wanted to get back on the plane with that emptiness in the belly, a slight hunger. With all her clothes on, she allowed herself a slight orgasm under his hand, went to bed alone, and put on her sundress to go with him to Denver the next day. The flight lasted an hour in clear weather.

Her lover at the time headed a pharmaceutical company but looked like André Malraux. He was married, somber, and French; he had an acid wit, with sunny periods when he talked about primitive art and about Africa, the continent where he'd done his military service and of which he'd retained some of the culture as well as the lust from which she benefitted. So much so that Hélène took herself for Josette Clotis, the happy and miserable mistress of Malraux, who granted her just time enough so he didn't become obnoxious, and who had been lucky enough to die young. He liked the comparison, she thought he would also love the children she'd give birth to for him at a distance, like Josette, but she would be careful not to die young. She had wings.

She started to tell her lover about it as soon as she got home, in mid-July. Their noon hours were generous, she prepared lunches of bread, wine, cheese, and grapes that could be eaten in bed and that seemed to make his sperm abundant. By stopping the pill at the end of the month, she said, there would be a chance of a baby in early spring and a maternity leave over the summer, a perfect arrangement for an academic. He let her talk, he smiled, a good sign in this brooder. July went on and on, humid and hot, he was greedier than usual, which was promising and arousing. At the beginning of August, on the last day of the heat wave, condoms suddenly appeared. He needed time to think things over, he said, which would be easier to do during a brief business trip he had to take, immediately, to Ukraine. He'd be back by September, when they would talk it all over. Nevertheless, he left the key to her apartment on the counter, he would not come back.

It is only in psychology books that one recovers from a love so sensual, from the embrace of an intelligent being. And Hélène didn't read them. Noon hours, she stifled in her office, alone. The nights were for sleeping pills and the daybreak was always too bright. There was cruelty in the eyes of every passerby, of all her colleagues and very much in those of the students who were starting the fall session. They seemed lighthearted. She detested them for taking up her time for grieving and she was even angrier with herself for having lost her lover over the idea of a child who would have resembled them one day. The evenings were blank, clear, filled with television.

When her publisher called to suggest a party to launch her book in October, she welcomed the tight deadline. She had to cut one hundred pages from a manuscript of three hundred and fifty; the price of paper was going up and today's readers don't want treatises. She had some arguments with the editor, which took up more slow hours. She put a great deal of care into approving the cover design, where she wanted a reproduction of Salome bearing aloft the head of John the Baptist, the forerunner. Her publisher maintained that a nonfiction book like hers shouldn't be illustrated, that it should be presented with a sober cover and that showing the decapitation, by a woman, of Saint John the Baptist, patron of the French-Canadian nation and consequently of the Québécois people, verged on symbolic provocation. But that was precisely what Hélène wanted, she had wings again, she was the hybrid who dares to stir up the sediment of all that is sacred. She would have a copy sent to James Carbonneau, with a note in English to thank him, even if he couldn't read the book. He'd figure it out.

She wasn't sleeping any better but, little by little, she was learning how to tolerate noon hour. The book party was a modest one. Hélène Pasquinel didn't belong to the first circle of Quebec historians, charming males but hard to convince of the significant role played by women in the course of the affairs of humankind. Lured by the title, *Partisan Women and Their Veils*, which could have been a book on discrimination against women inside political parties, the women representing chairs and departments of feminist studies were all present, however, as were those who edited specialized periodicals. There were also a few friends from boarding school with whom she had a drink at the Lion d'Or, courtesy of a publisher who found them all attractive. Perhaps, she thought on her way home, her life would now consist of writing, friends, and bistro sounds. Which would be fine.

The review in *Le Devoir* two weeks later was a massacre, and others followed. They said that her thesis, far from being audacious, was a contemporary version, insidious under its liberal appearance, of religious writings on the impurity of women. Not one living soul came to the defence of freedom of thought, even when the national council of the sovereignist party adopted a resolution at its fall meeting to condemn her regressive assumptions.

Hélène Pasquinel became better known. She was invited by an association of Catholics opposed to abortion to deliver the opening address at a conference.

She arranged with James Carbonneau, whom she called in Berkeley, to join him there for a few days to escape the poisons, get back on her feet, and try out her thesis on students who knew nothing about the passions of Quebeckers. The California winter was a summer, he said, she'd enjoy it. She no longer enjoyed anything but she settled with relief into a motel adjacent to the campus, where the TV discharged nothing but murders and declarations by one Clinton or the other.

James set aside a Sunday in San Francisco for her, he wore gloves to drive his ancient canary-yellow Camaro convertible, he knew every inch of the coast, he also sailed. She was expecting a lunch of mangoes, sweet chicken, and exotic salads in a pretty restaurant with a view; instead he took her to a Borders bookstore, to the nonfiction department, which seemed to her to be filled with kilometres of shelves. There were hundreds, thousands of books that no one had bothered to kill, he said. Most of them had been written by professors or researchers who had sacrificed hours of sun and sleep and Sundays like today. The pages of these volumes idled, they wouldn't be granted even the brief, waxy gaze museum visitors cast over everything that's not the *Mona Lisa*. At most, a Hélène Pasquinel or a James Carbonneau would read the jacket blurb one day before returning the book to alphabetical order and to the students who dusted bookstores part-time. Though he explained that this, not adverse reviews, was hell for an author, she regretted not seeing herself there, at peace among forgotten thinkers.

They bolted down quiche, salad, and cheesecake in the bookstore café, where nonsmokers were absorbed in the *New York Times*, each on his own, or hers. They were the only ones chatting sotto voce; she was filled with the torpor she'd read about in the novels of Magali that had thinned down her adolescent desires. The coffee was strong, James was a cloud, Hélène caught herself coming up with the English words to evoke her lover's departure. He talked at length, with his firm smile, about the meaning of "chutzpah," the Yiddish word that expresses something more than the notion of courage. She resigned herself to waiting, though right now she would have preferred to take consolation with James, whom she pictured naked in the narrow cradle of his sailboat. She brushed against his forearm and saw something like fine lines in the gaze of this man, who seemed to her to be gripped by the same desire. As in Aspen, he was in no hurry; it would be tonight. She was glad she'd brought the long dove-coloured silk nightgown that would go so well with a James and a semblance of summer.

He stopped outside the hotel around eight, the road had been silent, she didn't know if she should invite him for dinner, in turn, or find the words to bring him inside to her bed now, without breaking the thread of the day. He put his hand on her nape, rubbed it lightly, a prelude. "You know, Hélène, there is nothing I can do for you, really." He had a date later on, this Sunday, with his new lover, a fire-eater who earned his living repairing sailboats. For forty years now he had been savouring beautiful young men, students had broken his heart, but today it was no longer possible to touch them. Now and then he brushed up against women who reminded him of boys, like Hélène in Aspen, when she had wings. He looked at his watch, offered to drive her to the airport the next day.

Hélène Pasquinel disappeared six months ago; she now appears on a "missing persons" poster. In Montreal, her affairs are in a mess. But where she is, inside her head filled with water weeds that grow and multiply, no one will find her.

THE COLUMBARIUM

After she was burned alive
she took as a friend
the dove from the columbarium
They kept devastating the crypts
until the year two thousand
just time enough to waken sinners
with a belly's rose

She died on the eighth day of June, at seventeen past eleven, while reading the latest novel by Marie-Claire Blais. That is, she passed out on the nineteenth page of *These Festive Nights*, though it had nothing to do with the giddy round of that first long sentence wherein the novelist stirs up all the anxieties of this so-called fin-de-siècle. While her tender lover, the one who fixed the meals and gave her all the books, kissed her cold lips and her brow before calling the ambulance, she hadn't actually finished dying, though you wouldn't have noticed.

Something weird happened that no pathologist could have detected, even if an autopsy had been ordered, which was not the case.

Blais's characters, who were very disturbed and about to become even more so, hadn't taken into account the reader's death. How could they? Like fat houseflies that, come autumn, use guile to spend their final moments in the cracks of houses where the heat is coming on, the men and women had left the abandoned pages to attach themselves to the still-living brain of this woman who had been among the few to welcome them unreservedly. Beneath her temples the circumvolutions still gave off a fraternal warmth for them, whose development was not simple. They had followed her towards what they thought would be eternity.

And so Aurore, who had many friends, false and true, and a certain notoriety, had no awareness of her own funeral, which was the occasion for a huge quarrel. She had given birth to a perverse daughter and a naïve son; the one wanted to make her mother die for good, by inflicting on her the children's choir, the pallbearers, the flowers in the grimy church; the other saw her lying on silk on satin on oak, arms filled with the slender leaves of spring. Having no status, the lover couldn't get them to agree. Three days later, when the news of her death was getting around without the slightest notice in the papers, the undertaker imposed a ceremony that is still making tongues wag among the province's intelligentsia, a ritual in the garden on her property, under the very poplar tree where she'd been reading *These Festive Nights* during the first hot days.

Amid utter silence, to prevent a confrontation between the clans, part of the I Musici group, who had often enjoyed her editorial favour, played for eighteen minutes and thirteen seconds the *Partita for Strings Based on Chorales of the Evangelical Lutheran Church*, composed by Talivaldis Kenins, a Latvian-Canadian composer whose mother was a writer, his father, the translator of Baudelaire and Verlaine. And so, of the old-fashioned romantics and the depraved Catholics who were fighting over Aurore's remains, neither faction had won. But the ritual rang false, despite the perfect rendering of the music. For Aurore, Luther had been merely some youthful reading, in the same way as the God of the catechism, here being thanked in music. And Kenins was from Toronto, a place of no interest.

As she herself wasn't there, as her brain was jamming the airwaves and swarming still with the scraps of individuals it had had time to suck in during her final reading, none of that was of any importance to her whatsoever. And so it came to pass that she made the trip to the furnace, not even aware that her children had at least agreed on cremation and a niche in the columbarium, rather than a cemetery plot. In truth, she'd have liked to be buried under a huge tombstone in the shadow of the poplar, where the verdigris would have turned to moss till the end of time. But she had never said so.

So she went to the furnace. Without her daughter's delight or her son's terror, because neither of them knew, it turned out, that she was burned alive. For the body, it was only some small torture, the impression of disintegration she'd experienced so often in her dreams of airplanes in flames above the Atlantic, an endless orgasm that finally dried without ebbing, a venial sin there in the bowels that burned as slowly as green wood. The brain, however, went through hell. It was filled with furious beings who ought not to die save in the theory of the novel, who howled as they sought the exit from the labyrinth where gasses came rushing in, more blistering hot than the casket's shards. Some embraced before the end, others tore each other to shreds one last time; it was black and red and already ashen grey when Aurore made it through. She was the only spirit to escape the apocalypse, through grace because she had never believed in it. All the same, this time, by absorbing other people's woes from too close, she'd come close to staying there.

She shook the shreds of pages that clung to the wings of her spirit, which were white and made her a dove, as is proper. And she set out to take a look around while she was learning to fly.

Though summer was approaching it was cool. The numerous spirits that survive their bodies in columbariums are invisible; the site isn't designed for their comfort. The visitors, moreover, are well dressed, for cremation is a bourgeois custom. And above all they are rare.

When one's close relations are reduced to ashes and filed away in containers for the dead, it's not often that one misses their company. At most, here and there a plastic flower was suspended from a dead person's nameplate. Many were merely initials and dates that would not be erased, despite the desires of the living, for they were sheltered from bad weather.

For four years Aurore was bored in this greyness until a cortège similar to hers, except that the friends false and true spoke English, left an odour of sulphur around a plaque nearby. Marian had suffered only a little from the passage to the spirit world, she had no children and read mainly serious nonfiction, that is to say, intellectual games that presented no danger to the heart. Her own had failed one December 22 in the evening when she thought she was going to sleep on some mild wound to her self-esteem, which usually isn't fatal.

It was time they met, for they recognized one another, as happens in countries where some don't really speak the others' language, which fortunately forestalls the banality of reconciliations and yields works of suspicion, the strongest. "I've always loved you," said Marian to Aurore, whose public heresies had been an inspiration during her own break with the believers. They agreed during their first dusk as friends that God does not exist. As they were dead and fairly happy for eternity, it didn't disturb them in the least.

It was a very different matter for the guard who one April morning found two plaques that had come loose and, in place of the urns — one bronze, the other an iron alloy — found two parchments covered with very fine, very dark writing, one style upright, the other round, as if the author had been two separate hands.

As he was nearly illiterate, the guard left the documents with the police, who were surprised to find no sign of breaking and entering. Deciphered by a detective who had been literary before moving on to earn his livelihood by decoding the pitiful fictions recounted by suspects who are generally guilty, the texts showed themselves to be versions in French and English of a single story, one that was rather shameful for the two dead individuals, males close in age.

One was called Michel B., the other Herbert S. In the prime of their lives they'd been rather well known in the world of journalism and the law, and they'd rubbed shoulders from afar as activists on the then downright socialist left. Michel B. loved women and Herbert S. men but they had in common the fact that they concealed it, for the first was married and the second pretended to be. The manuscripts detailed cruel liaisons with high-class women they had nearly driven crazy.

The woman who had loved Michel B. had accepted the most dangerous clandestine meetings, long trips on stormy nights in cars that were falling to pieces, for quick backseat couplings. She had taken an indescribable pleasure from it, which he had diminished with an icy letter in the days that followed before he summoned her once again, according to his whim. He had extolled her intelligence as he was taking off her pants. As soon as she had believed they were made to get along in every respect, he had claimed to be swamped with work in court and had disappeared, but not before cashing the fee for the divorce he'd pleaded for her. Later on, he had received many honours, notably from progressive Christians who said that he was a good man.

The woman who had loved Herbert S. hadn't even experienced a heightening of the senses. A pressure on her fingers at most, in public, in the theatres or museums where he had showed off this woman who had a splendid shape if not a beautiful face, who was renowned for the brilliance of her prose. On the evenings of balls and galas, which had still taken place in this city that was just barely big, he had sometimes held her close in such a familiar way that people had said they were lovers. She had smiled, she had agreed, knowingly. She had assumed the sensual gaze of the satisfied woman. Every time she had hoped, every time he had gone home alone, without even brushing her cheek. Whenever she grew weary of this lie, which did happen, he had conjured up trips so that they'd finally be able to get used to each other, at leisure; they hadn't been one of those quick couples who sniff and consume one another right away. After two years, she had written him one of the most courageous love letters of the century. He had thrown it away with the leftovers of an elegant dinner in the company of a young man with an extravagant cock. She'd run into them the next day in a café, they were laughing, Herbert S. had kissed her hand then delicately wiped his lips, she was nothing but some faintly soiled foam at the end of a few wasted years. Besides, times were changing, he was soon able to be publicly gay, people found him interesting.

For several weeks the columbarium was closely watched. The guard no longer left the premises until he'd made the rounds of all the cupboards where some joker might have hidden to carry out some macabre farce, the locks had been changed, the incident was closed and unknown to the public at large, especially because the families of Michel B. and Herbert S. were most concerned that word not get around.

In October, when the most saffron of the autumn light came to lick the building's black granite, there were once again dead leaves near some empty urns. Again it was men with similar stories, this time less shocking, duller, too, for they were rather unknown or had become so. No one remembered Alexandre M., a minor poet, whose chapbooks were gathering dust in the Bibliothèque Nationale without ever having made their way into an anthology, while George L.

had flitted from translation to journalism as he dreamed of writing plays, leaving behind the vague memory of an intelligent failure. Anonymous authors reproached them not so much for having been parasites, which was undeniable, as for having domesticated the women who'd attached themselves to them. In both cases it was suggested, without indicating what work they had been immersed in, that these women could have become monuments of their century. Alexandre M. and George L. had given them the day-to-day happiness of which predatory loves had deprived them, had served them breakfast in bed, sent flowers, planned trips, seen to every dish for every candlelight dinner, cared for their minor aches and pains, carried their parcels, done the grocery shopping. That was how the women had filled out and stopped wanting to change the world, an attitude that had added more to the hearty stews to which they seemed to have contributed a lot. The men had died in bed, of repulsive, ordinary diseases. Even the memory of them had been a dead end for the women who had wasted several years of those that are said to be the best.

The detective, who was married to a rather hefty woman, found it hard to see what there was to criticize these solicitous lovers for.

He tried for some time to find a link between these men for, aside from the vague similarities in their lives, they moved in very different worlds. At the very most he found a mutual acquaintance, a foreign musician named Franz L., whose meetings with each of the men had occurred on separate continents and had been merely social. As for their families, they didn't even show up, one couldn't be found and the other couldn't have cared less.

One February day when the temperature was minus thirty-five, and despite the alarm that had been installed after the second incident, two cracked urns spread puddles of ashes onto the fake marble of the columbarium. The pages were sizzling hot, brief, and beautiful. Their literary quality was unrivalled, noted the detective who temporarily missed his old predilection. The deceased, Alfred M. and John C., at once despised, adored, and betrayed, had found themselves in Venice, a cliché of languor and light, on the balcony of a hotel room with a view of the Grand Canal. While one had been dying of dysentery and the other, in despair, had jumped into the iridescent water, some very beautiful women in the company of some very handsome Italian physicians had been looking for a way to save them. They had succeeded, more's the pity, because Alfred M. and John C. were perfidious and young and would haunt them once their male passion had abated.

The hotel's records having been burned, there is no way to elude the mystery that continued for years, until the year two thousand, in the crypts where no guard would set foot after dusk. Always, the lives of men who had sinned against women were restored in duplicate, revealing their worst flaws. There had been profiteers, lechers, rapists, and above all a long series of boring men who paradoxically had been the cruellest of all, for the women had been ashamed of yielding and embarrassed to go back to them.

The detective, who knew he belonged to that race, got the idea of appropriating the crime by turning the sheets of paper into a book, which was wildly successful under the title *A Belly's Rose/La rose au ventre*. The idea had come to him, he said, from what took the place of a signature, a hazy drawing of a woman's genitals which seemed to be printed in red chalk as a punctuation between stories. At length and in vain, he declared to all the interviewers, he had peered at this sign, which must be related to the authors' identity, but he'd had to conclude that what he was looking at was indeed the genitals of a woman, of two in fact, superimposed, which blurred the line and the message, too.

In a suburb of Montreal, a woman who read and re-read this amazing collection of stories, whose own life had been hollowed out by a long series of sinners, thought that in the drawing she had seen, rather, two Gs entwined. She had wit; her death was imminent.

THE KNIFE

If I cross my legs
says the woman he desires
You'll need a knife
Your hands will be cold
And I won't come

For a long time he had hesitated between a branch of the National Bank and one of the Caisse Populaire. From the vantage point of the church of Saint-Paul-de-la-Croix on Fleury Street, the first stood slantwise on the northeast corner and the second on the southwest side. The employees of the Caisse Populaire struck him as generally prettier but that could be just the effect of their skirts, which were very short and often pink and they wore them into fall if the weather was still warm. It's inappropriate to wear pale coloured, light cotton after September first in countries with a white, Christian tradition; until her recent death, his mother had been a strict observer of these rules, which were punctuated by Sunday Mass. But as he had always detested her and wished he had been the one who'd set the fire that had razed the retirement home and finally consumed her, she could not serve as a reference for his comparative assessment of the women from whom he intended to choose his wife.

If he had restricted his prospecting to the cashiers or clerks, it was because he was a math teacher in a public secondary school. There, he saw the budding of adolescents with little intellectual aptitude but, at times, great technical skills, who it pleased him to point in the direction of jobs that were humble but clean. To tell the truth, a number of the girls excited him, especially those who painted their nails in bright colours; for a while now he had even been seeing some that were lilac. It was a delight to watch them tapping away on a computer keyboard with their fingertips to protect their nail polish. He could observe their taut breasts, which he preferred small, he'd go into heat, though it didn't show. Never would he have touched one, even lightly. But he would marry one of their kind. It would be pleasant to do their accounts together, knees touching under the kitchen table, to plan carefully for a mortgage or a child, and to make love without having to talk too much, a talent he did not possess and dreaded in others. He had a small inheritance in addition to his savings, he was thirty years old, he was lying in wait and, though a virgin in spite of appearances, he wouldn't feel inhibited in the least. His solitary pleasure was based on the healthiest fantasies.

He had finally chosen the bank. The neighbourhood was mainly francophone and still had some characteristics of a village — the Caisse Populaire was overflowing with customers who went there the way they went to church, not so much to do business as to drop in for a chat, and who were perfectly content with the old-fashioned rhythm of transactions. This feature of civilization gave the young women who worked there a penchant for simpering, notably at elderly gentlemen who paid court to them pleasantly and with few repercussions. The premises were, therefore, rather crowded, even during slack periods, the ones that a teacher's timetable would have allowed him to take advantage of. The bank employees, by contrast, were more available, even though they were more reserved, notably in their dress, and it even struck him that they were slimmer, a nuance that was possible, though implicit, in the hiring policies of an establishment with puritan origins.

On the day after Labour Day he opened a chequing account and a savings account, after spending a summer observing. Slow walkers are less suspect when it's hot. Because the risk of holdups was higher at the bank than at the Caisse Populaire, which was too busy and had a more humble clientele, the women worked behind high bulletproof barriers that darkened their complexions. There were half a dozen of them, all brunettes, and he naturally went for the smallest because he himself was of average height and because her nail polish was a brown verging on pink, an elegant pearly hue that he'd never seen on his students. He was in no hurry. He only went to the bank once a week, around eleven a.m., and whether or not it was she who served him, he took notes on his way back to the apartment he rented on Sauriol Street, towards the west, one floor of a triplex he intended to buy from his aging landlord shortly.

Name, Julienne. Fine hair. Speaks softly. Myopic. Neat and tidy. Excellent posture. Wears a Swatch watch. Does not wear a ring.

When he'd finished his detailed account, which offered a very limited synthesis of Julienne, winter arrived, a month early. She started wearing black tights and fine knitted dresses, he never saw her in trousers, and that seemed to him to be the clearest sign of refinement. It was time to approach her and he did so rather stupidly, by asking her about interest rates, which were not her responsibility. As she was returning his updated bankbook, she gave him a crystalline smile he hadn't seen before. "Unless it's about my own rate of interest in men like you, Monsieur Lécuyer, I couldn't give you an answer."

He should have seized the moment, the last one available, to slip away, for it was abundantly clear that Julienne did not correspond to his notes, that she was an error of the kind that occurs when calculations have been too painstaking. But like many teachers he mistakes their vanity for the self-confidence the job requires. The bank was deserted. Before he was out on his own in the wet snow, with his failure, he made a couple of silly remarks to say he was flattered. The crystal became flesh, she would be at his place the next day, Saturday, at eleven o'clock, she said.

He left, skeptical. That evening, he made confetti of his notes. He felt like a writer at a dead end, at least as he imagined, for to him all literature was in a foreign language. He could have added some final words before filing them away. *She's crazy. A hooker. An extortionist. A nymphomaniac.* But all that was hypothetical and he hadn't skipped the social sciences for nothing. He was still free, if she did turn up, to pretend that he didn't understand or that he'd left for the country.

At eleven the next morning, he was, nevertheless, at the window watching a rusty Escort that he thought he'd seen before in the neighbourhood, where orange cars are rare, pull up in front of his door. She was wearing a fawn-coloured silk scarf with a short fur jacket that nearly slipped out of his fingers when he took it, so effectively did it combine softness, cold, the still-warm shape of the shoulders that offered themselves under a thin grey pullover, naked, as were her breasts, no doubt, he suspected they were erect. Her skirt was also grey and would have looked like a convent girl's were it not for the slit that ran up the right thigh nearly to the crotch, or to something lacy, he didn't dare to look.

She looked around while he was fixing coffee, as he wondered if she'd be taking her clothes off soon or later, and how he would react, because it struck him as dangerous to give in, though he didn't know why. "Like you, I take it black," she told him. She made her fine shoes waltz, settled into the best armchair, and started to tell him about Pierre Lécuyer, member of the teachers' union of the Montreal Catholic School Commission.

From just one reference number that she'd traced to the

next, she'd been able to draw up a report on a young man who was interesting in certain respects. Ten years earlier, at a time when those who were good with numbers were flocking to the faculties of management, he had chosen to enroll in the BA program in mathematics at the Université du Québec à Montréal, during one of those lucid periods that allow one to see what one's life might become. In the spaces between numbers, he guessed at the fullness of reason, his revenge over the superstition that had carried off his father, the hanged man, whose existence had been eaten away by scruples, by the pain of not having become a priest. Pierre Lécuyer was thirsty for data that were sharp, clear, blank. It wasn't his fault, to tell the truth, if none of his professors had at the time introduced him to philosophy, which was for the most part a form of calculation. Nor had it been his fault if he'd been able, thanks to student loans, to succeed without ever calling on the resources of the library and to decide, once his three years were completed, to call it a day and go and seek a brief pedagogical training that would let him earn a living.

His first credit card showed him to be cautious, except at an old record-dealer's, where over a period of eight to ten months he had assuaged a youthful passion for the old jazzmen whose improvisations were said to be mathematics raised to the level of genius, pure instinct. Then he'd had to furnish this apartment, which he'd done very well, as a matter of fact, he must have inherited his mother's taste for beautiful, durable things that transform spending into investing. The burgundy leather armchair where Julienne was sitting, for example, did not follow the current trend for soft pale cushions, it recalled, by stripping it bare, the form of the classic firm-skinned Voltaire chairs; one day it would make his heirs very happy.

Thus he had a sense of continuity, of the legacy that one never stops putting together if one is a responsible being. Indeed, it was what he had tried to inculcate in his mother when, at the end of sharp quarrels when she accused him no doubt of cultivating money in the way his father had cultivated remorse, he had finally persuaded her to leave the modest veterans' house on rue Christophe-Colomb that she'd lived in for thirty years, where repairs were becoming costly and the neighbourhood dangerous, prowlers having multiplied since a bike path had been put in. In the modest residence where she'd finally been put away, stubborn and unhappier than ever, she'd have preferred one of those over-looking the Rivière des Prairies, on the outskirts of Laval. It was hard to know how he'd managed to get himself appointed trustee of her possessions, since nothing in any medical or social records indicated that she'd lost the mental or physical capacity to administer them herself. One could not help suspecting that beneath her son's apparent affability lay some form of blackmail to protect the estate. The old lady's expenditures were very limited, as were her outings. The sum she had left corresponded precisely to the city's evaluation of the house on Sauriol Street. It wasn't a fortune but a tidy nest egg for a thirty-year-old man with no other obligations, not even a car loan.

A son more economical than his mother is rare but possible, especially if he has a good knowledge of mathematics. This episode then could testify to a reasonable personality — a man making provisions for the future as a citizen who refuses to rely on the state's resources. The only benefit he would accept from the state would be the result of his subscription to Lotomatique, an odd choice for someone with such a logical mind, but we all have our contradictions and that one is relatively minor. As for the meanness some people might have suspected to be at work in the planning of his inheritance, it was, all the same, refuted by the deduction at source that the teacher authorized to make monthly payments for an annual contribution of two hundred and fifty dollars to Centraide, an amount well above the average donation.

Every year, his name could also be found on the lists made public by the director general of elections because of a one-hundred-dollar gift to the Parti Québécois, which would quite naturally receive less than the poor. For a while, after his university years, he was also to be found on the executive of his Péquiste riding association, where he was, of course, treasurer. It's hard to verify why his membership was softer now. He seemed to stand on the anonymous curve in the polls where, as one ages, fear of change naturally takes precedence over any desire to correct errors of fate. At least he still contributed to the party coffers, which could lead one to assume that he'd voted OUI in the 1995 referendum and that, while leaving it to others to further the cause, he wasn't blocking the movement.

As he was not known to subscribe to any newspaper or magazine, it was hard to follow the slope of his other ideas and it was possible that he didn't have any, which was Julienne's assumption. This she sweetened with a smile as she poured herself the rest of the coffee. At half-past noon, daylight was still refusing to pour in through the windows, though they were quite huge.

It was undeniable as well, this she could say out loud, that Pierre Lécuyer was rather good-looking and healthy as a horse, as was attested once a year by the local medical clinic and, above all, by his file at the downtown branch of the YMCA, where he gave his muscles a workout for less than it would cost at a Nautilus centre. The girl who'd assessed him when he enrolled must have been impressed. She had itemized his strength, his slimness, his cardiovascular resistance with a care that showed admiration and perhaps desire. He had smooth clear skin, normal hair coverage, and a birthmark in the small of his back that a woman would undoubtedly find attractive and at the same time a powerful stimulus to lust.

Now she was finished, the coffee, too. Her lips were still quivering, she had pearly fingernails, and he would have felt them on his soul if he'd had anything resembling one. He was naked under Julienne's words, she had to take him, he wanted it, never till this day had he desired anything. She smiled, sitting erect, her legs still crossed at the knees. If she were to open herself to a normal member of the male species, she told him, he would have to use a knife. "Your hands will be cold and I won't come."

She went forth. He had a knife but it was steady and he used it cautiously.

THE SONG

I set fire to the covered bridge
and left you on the other shore
where there's not a living soul
I hear your cry
I have engraved it
Solo for a dying lover
The opera companies keep asking for more

During strawberry season you stained your white blouse, just at the third mother-of-pearl button. You buttoned it to the collar, even in summer, to protect your throat and your trills. I had told you to be careful, you must wash strawberries before you hull them, otherwise they bleed. You never listened to me. I repeated that you have a tiny brain, and that it would dry up on the day you lost your golden voice. You shuddered. I hate to see the water moving in your eyes, which are the eyes of a frightened perch. I had charged you to set aside your soul for the individuals at the concert; they believed in it, I didn't.

On the left and above your breast, which was so small, they say that's a sign of intelligence though I doubt it, there was then a pink stain, a woman's grease mark in the wrong place and at the wrong time of the month. I thought your blood must be pale as well, washed out, sugary. I got the idea of popping the buttons, of stabbing you to the heart, which would not have resisted long, I knew it was weak. There was a nick in the strawberry knife, there was a risk of damage. I restrained myself. I wouldn't go to prison for so slight a matter as you.

You sang better when I filled you with gloom. I made you begin again for the thirteenth time the recitative of Adalgise from the first act of *Norma*, and you were finally able to stay on key. You'd never be Callas and you'd always sing maids, but today's songs are for second voices. The composers alone are gods, it is their sound that we acclaim.

Then it was one p.m. at the end of a springtime of variable skies. We were in the forlorn city, the city that was born of a razed forest and icy water. All that was left was a piano in the school where the teacher was beautiful and brunette with very heavy breasts and the neck of a whore. I would take her from behind, hers was broad and good.

I smiled at you for the first time that day, I reminded you of the harbour where I'd met you, a blonde Adalgisa who was serving beer on board the yachts and who sang *Summertime* for dullards on vacation. Who first spotted you, insignificant bird? I had an expert eye and a firm hand, you did well to follow me and you followed me again through the forlorn city. I ordered you to change your blouse. You were wearing ecru linen, you were nearly pretty in the middle of the day, but my cock no longer responded. So it goes.

You asked why I'd rolled down the windows, something I didn't allow when you were going to sing. I said that there had never been such a hot springtime, that we were driving in the wind, that the air was cut off. We took the dirt road where the grass grew thick in the ruts, you were frightened by a fox with rabid eyes that shot by, I made you keep quiet, featherbrains are afraid of everything. We stopped in a clearing strewn with hunters' cartridge cases, where they told each other about the deer they hadn't killed and the women they hadn't had but they'd have them in the South, once their money came in. They had all moved on, they'd left the forlorn town, their worn and faded wives. They were wrecks who slept with other wrecks around de Bullion Street. One of them had shown me the road, the clearing with the cartridge cases and the island that doesn't appear on maps. He had told me amid the blare of a night of jazz, I remembered it with the roar of the trumpet that came within a hair's breadth of an apocalyptic note, I was the only one who'd heard it. You knew better than anyone that no musical notation had any secrets from me, even though I've never been able to sing.

I broke ferns, made a bed under the aspens, spread a pink sheet, but it wasn't to make love to you. We drank lukewarm water, downed some stale bread and cheese that had gone bad. Wine didn't make it up to the town, nor did pâtés or pastries. People there ate only bony pike and partridge soured in butter. You wanted to go home but you had to listen to me, I needed to make you hear all the voices of the forest, from the bee drowned in loosestrife to the snake crumpled under the debris of an old casting. There is a similar place in Italy, where Rossini collected every note of his solemn low mass, I told you, and I expected that you in turn would learn them all. I would give you the time, the summer had hardly begun. You didn't think it possible to submit your voice to such sounds but I was the master. You were successful with the song of the robin; the most inane of birds, it sometimes can't find its own nest, it cries out in the middle of the scale, a clear, lackluster *fa* that will never be sharp or flat. You had an amazing talent for the *fa*, a note of abasement that's of no interest to divas.

Two hours passed with my words. You listened, you didn't know what I was getting at. I showed you. We left the clearing and the remains of the meal to the raccoons that lay in wait for human garbage. The grass on the road, now barely visible, was tall, it grazed your knees, there was a long turn where I held your hand to make you think we were still together.

The river spoke before you saw it, it crackled over rusty gravel, it was celebrating you, it hadn't had a female friend for so long, it was brown and green and thought itself beautiful but it was rotten with algae and the excrement of the forlorn city, only perch survived there, and the carp that no fishermen wanted.

Along the way we saw the covered bridge. The river, still high, licked the huge joists that jutted out past its body, once painted red but now washed out like the so-called polychromatic statues in museums. We crossed it ten times, from shore to shore. The echo of our footsteps was lost in the sultry heat that oozed from its framework, riveted for eternity. Along its length, at shoulder height, windows opened onto the middle of the water, a broken silence entered and was glass between us. It was you who spied the cross of Lorraine carved on either side of the central pillar and the graffito: "le jour de gloire est arrivé." I touched your nape in confirmation of the sign; you were about to conquer France by offering her the most forgotten and the newest sounds of her former colony, they would run out of birds' names to celebrate you in their newspapers, where flattery is written so beautifully. You were smiling, I didn't know if it was because of the caress or the glory, I'd gambled on both of them to make you sing.

The other shore was the island. It had no name, the hunter had told me. And so I couldn't give it yours, Adalgise. It was made of moss and resiniferous trees driven there by the waves, it was easy to run in that place. I dazed you there in the sunlight, then I told you, as I peered at the rare shadows, that the east was in the west and the north in the south. You believed me, you knew nothing, daughter of Hochelaga's sidewalks. I laid you down in the lichen, I ordered you to nap as I caressed you under your short skirt, you opened up under my fingers, viscous languor, and I left you there.

You slept, I'm sure of it, while I was taking in the covered bridge, while gasoline fumes mingled with the grime on the wood, while a worried deer scampered past nearby. And as the match flared, a single one that kindled the beams with a glow that crept on and on, before the sparks. The fire was icy yellow, filigree in the clear sky. When the roof collapsed onto the roadway, it dug a trench, I swear I saw the cross of Lorraine shine mauve before it drowned. I left. I turned my back on you while whistling *La Marseillaise*, the heroic deeds were burned.

I came back at midnight. Segments of glowing embers clung to the two shores, like a midsummer celebration in the land of ghosts. I sat upstream amid bulrushes whose velvet smelled like incense, there are many oils in the wood of old bridges and some may be blessed, because there was a time when bridges used to be baptized. Cold vapour rose from the water, I could barely make you out, standing by a fir tree dead that very day, by my hand. Your image trembled in the forced heat. Then you turned your back, you disappeared into the island, for hours there was only the hissing of the water as it devoured the last of the fire; now the smoke smelled like wet cigarettes. I thought I saw your bright shadow dance behind that curtain but you wouldn't dare, you only dance when tipsy and we hadn't drunk.

Then you did what I'd been waiting for. First the muttered prayers. You modulated the litany of the dead, you still believed in God, that would soon end, while I fell asleep on my bed of reeds, I took full advantage of it. When I woke up the air above the rubble was crystalline, the fire had washed the waves, your singing would be pure.

For three days, I recorded everything on tape. You were trying to placate me, you knew I was lurking on the side of the living. You repeated all the notes, from the bee's buzzing to the silk sound of the snake, the squealing, the cawing, the stridency — all the way to the perfect flat note of the wind in the tundra that began here, on your island, Adalgise. It is death in life, in green, in swarming verses.

You reappeared at the river's edge, you were looking for me, you were hungry, cold, your skirt was stained with black from the covered bridge and your complexion, by the clouds that were arriving for the requiem. It was then that you fulfilled all my hopes, that I loved you with a vivid love, as if you were finally my daughter, carried off by a long illness, my personal tragedy, I who wanted one so badly. You cried all day long, howling and then submissive, in a major decrescendo the likes of which we shall not hear again among the living. Then you lay down on your stomach, I gathered your hiccups, they seemed to emerge from your dark shoulders. I think you finally fell asleep, the lichen would give you the dreams you needed for dying while you were thinking I would take you back.

Sleep this summer, Adalgise, die before the winter, which is very harsh in this land. Let it embalm you with ice, you will be beautiful still when some individual sails by in a small craft and finds you in the spring, hardly mutilated, loved by the flies and the breezes at ground level. I shall be far away and unknown in these parts, where no one remembers a covered bridge.

I went back to my populated town. You had caught cold, I said, and you wouldn't sing again, we'd split up one midsummer eve. For a long time I went around, to first performances and last ones, with the look of a lover who was distraught and perhaps deceived. A singer consoled me, she was twice your age and I finally filled all the space between her hips, I exhausted myself there. When all that was left of me was the genius, I worked at combining all your sounds, I carved out the most desperate ones more clearly, I set down the simple, tearful ones in the background and I inserted pauses from your scattered silences. The heaviest one was the last.

I produced *Solo for a Dying Lover*. An expert recorded it on a fashionable label, others would have killed to be singled out there. Germany and Italy greet the sounds of an obscure composer, they hear the fire smouldering under my fingers — so it's said in the newspapers where reputations are made. The opera companies keep asking for more. Now that I think of it, I should have saved you on the seventh day, when I was God. Instead of which I am damned. My heroic deeds have all been burned.

THE LOVERS

My lovers die ugly and cold
I live to forget them
I was a hundred years old when the last one moved on,
the wily one who excelled at causing pain
He was handsome, I'd already killed him

To say that the first was my lover would be going too far and would suggest, incorrectly, a form of incest, because he brought me into the world and I don't know if he ever desired me.

For Léon Burelle, I was a classroom exercise, even though his vocation had already been ensured during his fourth stay in the France of his ancestors. The man had good reason for being melancholy and for wanting to get away from it all. The good burghers whose portraits he painted repelled him. The churches he decorated would be destroyed in the next century. His many children were angry with him for having killed their mother. The artistic theories of Hippolyte Flandrin were mocked. Léon Burelle's life expectancy was only about twenty years.

And so it was unlikely that he would live to see the completion of the great basilica on Montmartre that the Republic and the archbishops intended to dedicate to the Sacred Heart as a sign of national contrition for the troubles during the Commune. Work on it had slowed down after the death of Abadie, the architect, and the foremen had shilly-shallied for so long before digging the foundations in a layer of gypsum that the façade facing Paris wasn't finished yet.

Léon Burelle was particularly interested in the nave, which would need another ten years before it took shape. He sloshed through the lava-like mud spat out by the worksite, timidly questioned the workers, spent more than two hours going home by omnibus or by steam-powered tramways packed with damp-haired working girls. Everywhere the streets were blocked by the building sites for train stations that were going up much faster than the church, thanks to some clever tricks with iron and glass. On the Place d'Enfer, which no one could get used to calling Denfert-Rochereau, in a *pension* that smelled of the fat woman who ran it, he dined on boiled beef and a glass of clarified burgundy, his stomach churning from a touch of enteritis he correctly attributed to the water that came from a river filled with suicides. He spent the evening drawing up requests for interviews with architects or craftsmen known to be inspired by religion. Their influence was declining, but they measured the hours of their winter and this Canadian did not strike them as somebody useful.

And so he was elated, filled with gratitude, and in a state of heat that may have contributed to my birth, when he found himself with Jean-Baptiste Faure, a baritone at the Opéra, who had composed *Rameaux* and *Crucifix*. Plump, loud, endowed with a charmingly modest wife and an apartment in which velvet caskets held paintings in the antique heroic style that had launched the century so well, M. Faure must have talked to him about the survival of Christian themes in republican art. Was he stricken with pity, or friendship, for this man in a frock coat as outdated as his accent, frail in body and in beard, who had surely never touched a dancing girl? In any event, it happened that after his wife had withdrawn, over a cigar and cognac and amid the dampness of a conversation that slipped from arches and centres to the grace of the Magdalenes on Calvary, Jean-Baptiste Faure disclosed to Léon Burelle his collection of Courbets: three erotic paintings whose morality is still disputed to this day.

There was the painting that would become more famous perhaps than the *Mona Lisa*. It was not yet called *The Origin of the World*, its fleshy female genitals painted faceout, if I may put it that way, but without a face. Léon had never seen the genitals of his own wife, which were perpetually hidden by a woollen dress or a nightgown, as was customary in French Canada at the time. He did not know if these were fresh or if they resembled what he would have seen on a wife who was dying from too many pregnancies. Burelle's gaze was uncorrupted and Faure understood from the long silence that his guest was sparing him. Certainly they were communing.

I was born on the following day, in the first glimmers of a dawn that was finally sunny, in the secrecy of a roomette in the *pension* on the Place d'Enfer, before Léon had washed his face and his backside with the cold water from the ewer placed at his door. I am a copy of *The Origin of the World*, a red chalk drawing carefully executed from memory by Léon Burelle whose own was precise.

Immodesty having been admitted in my case, I declare myself to be more seductive than the original. I am all shuddering rosy pink, from the most enticing to the weariest, from the areola of my one visible breast to my clitoris, in varying states of arousal, from the shadow I make on the page to the one that appears in my cleft. The Impressionists, whom my creator abhorred, have turned pink into a colour that murmurs. The pink that Léon Burelle placed in the origin of the world, one March morning that he felt all the way to his icy fingers, is that of the embers of damnation.

Was he himself aroused by it? I don't think so. I have not often felt his gaze on me. He stowed me in his baggage along with some more biblical copies, including that of a Salome utterly frigid beneath her veils. He seemed to have grasped nothing yet about the flesh. Conversely, we may assume that his obsession till the end with excessively covering his nymphs and his female saints could be a defence against the agitation I afforded him, even when buried under mountains of sketches. I've always had a great deal of presence.

And so I caught the attention of a young researcher appointed to sort out the artist's records after Léon Burelle's death, who was astounded to see me appear from between the pages of an album of nude photos that had nothing scandalous about them, for they were academic poses, which Christian artists were permitted to study as long as they abstained from any lewd interpretation. Inquisitive minds such as Kenneth Clark's, who much later and with a great deal of circumlocution distinguished between the nude and nudity, said nothing more than our pastors. The boy, whose name was Hervé Magnan, who'd been brought up in the country, who'd been educated by the ways of animals and priests, was one of those whose virginity weighed heavily on him. He stole me for his personal use, a heresy in the eyes of art history, but I believe his deed conforms with Burelle's underlying wishes. He would have made me disappear if he'd thought about it in the course of his final hours, saturated with so many torrents of piety.

I had with young Hervé a very simple, too brief relationship, for which I still have a yearning. At the time, it was impossible for a common man who was unfamiliar with the few dives in our towns and who had never travelled to have in his possession any lewd images of some robustness. My own image, which was superior for triggering an erection, had the advantage, moreover, of having been acquired on the job, in a Christian setting, which diminished the guilt normally associated with solitary pleasure. Thus I saw with the moistened eye I have between my thighs some touching scenes wherein the ardour was purely for reasons of health. I've never found anything similar since, nor have I regretted having been for that belated pubescent a mere object.

What I liked about him was equally circumscribed.

Our innocence was brief, of course. Thanks to the sexual confidence I developed in him, the young man set about to dream of other friendly flesh and I had no way to warn him about the difficulties, more frequent than one might imagine, of attaining sensual pleasure in company. And so he became attached in succession to two or three school teachers, one of whom was passionate enough to let him glimpse a nipple, which resembled mine, and that resulted in marriage. At the time he was earning a modest livelihood at the Musée du Séminaire de Québec, sorting out the nuns' collections. It was impossible for him to introduce me to his superiors and equally impossible, out of professional conscience, to relinquish me altogether. At least he had the happy idea of writing a note about my provenance, along with a detailed description of my measurements and my composition, a monograph not unworthy of the structural grammar being used in art schools today. He filed it among the documentation on some vessels more sacred than mine. No one would consult it for years. And I was abandoned in that company, between sheets of tissue paper, far from the light that is fatal to drawings, particularly those in red chalk. And that is how the history of art in Quebec is indebted to Hervé Magnan for my preservation under the finest museum conditions, for the undeniable proof that I am part of the work of Léon Burelle, and for the certificate of authenticity that would ensure, with my growing popularity, the fortune of my future lovers. All that was missing was my connection with *The Origin of the World*, which would long remain unknown. For the rest, posterity has conserved none of Magnan's works, he died in obscurity after a conventional union with a woman who was lacklustre in bed. I can't feel sorry for him, he'd had a choice.

I experienced fifteen years of rest. Then I met the man I shall call here the churchwarden, to respect the anonymity allowed him by the greatest journalist in Quebec when he introduced the churchwarden in May and June 1964, in columns in *Maclean's*. Voyeurs can stop here, our relationship was platonic. And above all tragic.

The churchwarden was in the prime of life and his powerfully religious background had forged his nonbelief. In a small provincial town where the atheism of a leading citizen would create a scandal, so he thought at any rate and tried to protect his family from such a thing, he struggled endlessly with himself, disgusted by his lie and indignant at the circles that forced him into it. The journalist recalled a night during the forties when the two had met, an unlikely pair, in a house that was dozing under the hypocritical whiteness of December.

They drink, luckily. They are associates in their all too private rejection of a Quebec dazed by its fear of God. The churchwarden unlocks a bookcase, opens his Hell to the visitor — dozens of books whose only wrong was to allot more space to reason than to faith.

I was there, I tell you. But the churchwarden dared not introduce me to the exquisitely sensitive man who stood before him, a being who was not unfamiliar with the flesh, who would undoubtedly have understood and taken an interest in the image that had come from the very depths of Léon Burelle's soul. A cry of vengeance against the colours of a life thinned by the water of penitence. Against gazes lowered in the presence of forbidden paintings. Against the weakness in the knees of their people, where their anger submits.

I was there between them, I preferred to hear their voices rather than touch their eyes, they didn't need my presence to know my unbearable secret.

That night the churchwarden came to the end of his despair and decided to sell me. I didn't belong to him, as you know, I had entered his house in guilty fashion, which added to his perpetual remorse. He was educated, the curé had entrusted to him the task of finding information about the parish chalice, which was thought to be from Ranvoysé; the church councils were beginning to assign some value to their liturgical objects even if it was only with a view to selling them to connoisseurs whose offers for such relics seemed stupendous. The churchwarden had unearthed me in the Magnan archives at the Musée du Séminaire, he had related his discovery of me to a scandalized cleric who undoubtedly would have destroyed me if the village notable hadn't offered to purge the premises, to keep the terrible discovery a secret.

All the years he spent becoming slowly drunk, the church-warden also spent looking for a buyer. In Montreal, the groups of young people who had made Alfred Pellan their master gladly found in eroticism a banner for their move-ment. But my owner was from another age and he'd never looked at me with a lascivious eye. I was the flesh, the transubstantiation of his grief, he wanted to leave me with-out hurting me. And he feared that the work of Burelle would be scoffed at in these groups, seen as a symbol of the hypocrisy of yesterday's artists, who were being repudiated in wholesale quantities.

The vicar who paid him regular visits when he was no longer a churchwarden and disease had announced that extreme unction was imminent, was a strange lad. Tall, corpulent, chubby-faced, he often replaced the Roman collar with a turtleneck and it was easy to see his disappointment at being posted to a parish that was still asleep and even hostile to the first echoes of the Quiet Revolution. In this weakened notable, whose confession he quickly abandoned any thought of hearing, he found a confidant. Their exchanges were at a lower level than those on the famous night in December, which the journalist had in fact not yet described. The vicar was one of those more worked on by the flesh than by the spirit; he granted the old man's indulgence as testimony to the agitation he himself felt as he fulfilled his pastoral duties among the normal school students who boarded at the school, the eldest of whom had given him to understand that the vicar's religious office would be no obstacle to more intimate relations. The sick man, who had so much wanted not to conceal anything when he was the other man's age, encouraged him to leave the priesthood. The priest shrank back, calling upon a faith that he maintained did still exist and his duty as a moral guide to ordinary souls. He defended his right to go on teaching and to offer the sacraments even as he authorized himself some forbidden acts, thereby placing himself above his own teaching through the grace that God had given him to confide a variable interpretation of his Word.

The former churchwarden was fascinated by this verbose duplicity which, under the appearance of modernity, brought back to us the customs of the abbots of the court. He had an image of the long line of ecclesiastics who had broken their vows but would cling to their privileges, trying to hold on to the Word and even to remain the arbiters of earthly lives. The vicar's weakness seemed to him an extension of his own; he liked and at the same time despised the vicar, and the churchwarden no longer had any other company. He offered the vicar mine, for a few hundred dollars that were immediately passed on to some charitable works.

To me, the churchwarden's end, weary and resigned, was appalling. In a pitiful way, it marked my own entrance into the world.

The vicar had found in me the perfect pivot for moving on to his new vocation without giving up the advantages of the old. I was a fine piece for a dissertation, I'd been drawn by the hand of a master, I had a history and a literature. And I was also a gorgeous cunt. He had me circulated first in secret, in black satchels, among others like him, who camouflaged their temptations behind theses teeming with clichés about the *Song of Songs*. The caution of Léon Burelle, a man of churches, was all the more fortunate because it coincided with a return to our cultural roots, to fishing nets and farm furniture, which would help stir up a new nationalism. I became the secret, widely shared, of the sexologists — new priests who in many cases proceeded from the old ones — who established their presbyteries in university faculties. The lovemaking I often inspired, dressed up as therapy, both delighted and saddened my eye; misery won out over exultation, and too many young women wept because they did not look like me — of whom it was slanderously said that I offered myself unrestrainedly.

I hated that man, the vicar. My revenge was to see him become a eunuch, his fat swelling along with the money that was my salvation, or so I thought.

Although my photo had been reproduced in several sex manuals, I had never been exhibited. An avant-garde gallery owner spotted me at my owner's, whose influence was beginning to decline in a Quebec where people were now having sex outside of marriage, even on the TV soaps. He seized the opportunity to return to the spotlight, then to receive the attractive sum offered by a young collector, a wealthy man as rich as he was handsome.

I was so glad to leave those big paws for slender hands that I didn't watch the transaction. For a few months I was content, in an attractive study adjacent to his vast downtown office, one entire floor of a building designed by Mies van der Rohe, no less. I was bathed in indirect light, conservation *oblige*, but it was a blue lined with mauve, which suited my complexion perfectly. I found there the affectionate humour of *The Origin of the World*, I emitted desire, it sometimes happened that I woke up filled with lust, that I sang.

In the end I realized that it was in vain. The friends he invited into the study, who shared his costly scotch while discussing art or business or both, caressed me only with the eyes of connoisseurs from which any carnal appetite was absent, as it was from the eyes of my master. Were they indifferent to women or were they mere temple merchants to whom today's artists are reduced to selling their souls? I couldn't say, though I have my own ideas.

I was obliged to admire in spite of myself, however, the person who had appended me to his life, who exploited me thoroughly by refusing to let himself be seduced, who was thought of, henceforth, as the best-informed collector in Quebec, whose artistic audacity let you forget his greedy nature, even in the eyes of our most destitute artists.

Justice does exist. On the day of my one hundredth birthday, which he hadn't pointed out because of my own indifference to that milestone, he was found on the pearl-grey carpet in his study with his throat slit, eyes still open, focused on my cleft. I am the only one who knows who did the deed, an ordinary man whom I'd bewitched, who had been charged with keeping me beautiful, who caressed me at night with a cloth before emptying my master's garbage cans and scraping off his dust.

When he cut the good-looking boy's jugular vein, he forced the collector to look at me, he told him of the fierce and fragile joy of a woman's sex. And told him he had to kill him before he had my skin, before I became, under glass, *Untitled, red chalk drawing, Léon Burelle, 1888.*

Which I am.

Tomorrow I go into the museum, I wipe out part of the taxes on the estate. I shall have thousands of lovers, who will think I'm alive and whom I'll deceive.

PURGATORY

Her yellow dress slipped onto the flagstones of penitence
"Forgive me, Lord, for having heard you moan
behind this red curtain."
He clad her in his own black frock
They took that day's flight to a new-found land
where for a time they were happy

The dancing rapid rushes at the foot of a church that is fifty years old, more or less. The car skids onto the gravel, a woman who always visits deserted churches stops and that's why it is noon.

The dancing rapid has the summer before it, the river has been a little lower ever since the parishioners cleared its bed of the round stones from which they built a church, she read that in the tourist guide to Abitibi-Témiscamingue. She has round knees and her shoulders are round as well, she'd have been a beautiful stone made to endure under water, she'd have refused to end up cemented by their trowels to the ugliest glory of God, who has never come here. The workers realized that once the front steps had been finished, when the first bride ran away on the eve of her wedding and the village aborted its last child.

The dancing rapid drops into a river that silences its music. There's a bend in the river where lonely men fish for cancerous pike, they have built their supply post beyond the reach of harmonium or incense, they drink their beer from cans that they toss onto the shore where the dancing rapid dies.

The portal is open. It remains open when Élise crosses the threshold. She glides across the grey linoleum. She has never seen anything like it. Plastic carnations under each of the Stations of the Cross, charcoal drawings on yellowing laid paper framed in plastic. A profusion of paper roses around the plywood altar, around the plywood of the balustrades, the pews, the staircase to the rood screen — poor people's wood painted sky blue. A lit bare bulb above a bulletin board. *Donations welcome, we still have to build the steeple.* A fierce-eyed plaster angel stands near the lectern for sermons, he is crushing a snake with a broken forked tongue. Élise feels friendly towards demons conquered by the toes of angels, who are all killers. She's met a good many in deserted churches.

The aisles are steeped in the smell of ammonia, here nothing turns to dust, she has found the spot for reflecting on purgatory, sitting erect in the last blue pew, her back to the extinguished vigil lights.

Her husband is in purgatory. He died two weeks ago. He was ploughing the belly of a woman golfer on an overly soft bed in a motel along the TransCanada Highway. Siestas there are sold for sixteen ninety-five. They'd been hitting balls since dawn, you can understand the hunger that is born on a level with the holes while the sun beats down and calves turn red. He was weary, the golfer relentless, it had been a long time since Élise put this man's heart at risk. In bed he was cold and incompetent, it was pointless for Élise to perfume herself for such brief urges. The day would come when she would buy silk petticoats with lace bodices for a man who would take the time to capsize with her on stormy carpets. Her summer was ahead of her. She was grateful to the golfer all the same, she wouldn't have wanted to live with the memory of a death rattle at her neck, of the dread in her husband's eyes. He had spared her the horror, she had nothing for which to forgive him, she'd had him burned dry. And now he was in purgatory and she had to think about it, for each of us has his own way of mourning.

Purgatory is a place all made of wax. On the right, at the front, the virgin is naked. On the left, joseph is naked and virgin. In the middle, the jesus of Prague is a perpetual dwarf under a ruby cope and a crown stiffened with gold leaf.

The holy family stares out blankly at the long pews similar to those in the dancing rapid's church, where are stored the shadows of flawless sinners who will never touch one another. A fine rain falls onto their grey bodies. Once a day a slaughtering angel quenches them with still water so they can wait longer and not despair of the light, they can hear only the sound of it, a crystalline sound that looms up out of nowhere. After a century the rain becomes scalding, the wax melts, the shadows leave their places one by one, and go to a place where a meal will be offered.

Élise's husband will fade away with his memory, she bids him goodbye as she did every morning when he got into his grey car, his head filled with numbers, his hand, with a telephone. Yesterday she bought a lilac-coloured car with upholstery of burnt barley, today she donned a long yellow dress over a silk petticoat with a lace bodice; there are a hundred-odd kilometres between her house and this stop in purgatory where she has to spend time before living.

Half-past noon. Nothing moves. She will melt a little wax, a vigil light, to help the shade that was hers to move towards the light. She hasn't a cent for a donation. Into the slot she drops her wedding ring, it's worth as much as the spire on the steeple. It falls and clinks with a very soft moan.

Which persists. And rises in spurts. Élise turns without a sound, she thinks she sees the confessional's red velvet curtain move, it is suspended from a roughly rounded wooden rod, the limp enclave is closed on the right side by latticework, the kind used for enclosing pergolas. The kneeling bench is vinyl, red as well. Someone is crying behind the velvet, the lamentation is more distinct now, it is tender and moist, it has the hoarse sweetness of a violin trying to set the tone and persisting, only to spit out the wrong note. Élise bends and leans into the shadow, it's been so long since she was penitent like this, it goes back to the first sin of the flesh, which she never regretted, but suddenly she misses the blank murmuring among strangers, made up of the permitted lies. She holds her breath but the black panting form can hear nothing, now she is merely untidy flesh and if daylight should enter the deserted church Élise would see the final contortion of a sad orgasm. She allows the final flayed *A* to emerge from the throat of the man in black before she interrupts the sighs, slower now:

"Forgive me, Lord, for having heard you moan behind this red curtain." He is not startled. "I knew you were beside me, Madame."

For a long time they stay there, she kneeling, he leaning towards her, taking pleasure in the story of evil that has just gushed cold.

The church had been deserted for two years and would remain so. He was the last of the oblates but the one least bruised, the one who could be assigned twelve churches in the countryside and the forest and would not complain. For that would entail the same number of confessionals in which to dream of hearing sins, which was what he'd wanted when he took his vows. No one came there now to prostrate themselves, but still he sat from day to day and recited the sins of the absent penitents. It was easy to do while he read the morning paper. Yesterday, he'd heard the rapist with the scythe, the one who surprised little girls in the strawberry fields and cut them so delicately that they fell asleep very gently when their blood had run out. But also the accountant who'd had his wife passed off as a thief and she believed him, and confessed before her children. And then the madwoman, the same one three times, who broke the hammers of pianos to make touring musicians weep and the last pleasures of the villages vanish.

He judged them, he enjoyed judging them before he imposed on them different ways to make a fresh start, to cut little girls with stilettos, to kill wives with words, to burn the wood of guitars, which could have replaced the pianos. Today, there was no newspaper. Was she aware of that? No, she doesn't read newspapers, she's afraid of turning up in one herself, dead before her time, you never know. "You're mistaken, Madame, for I invented one that you were in, on the front page, this very morning." He'd had a black coffee, he had foreseen a woman in a long yellow dress who would commit a sacrilege in the church of the dancing rapid while she listened to him come under the eye of god. "You are my accomplice, Madame." He explains complicity to her. The most perfect kind existed only in the confessionals where the man in black was a receptacle for poisons, until he got drunk on depravity and lost his awareness of beings. The complicity disappeared with the penitents who went away, who, henceforth, confide in their friends, the police, and the papers. But how would a priestess in a yellow dress be set free without the state of grace? She would be forever covered with the odour that rises between them. "An angel perspired, Madame, and you must impose upon him a different way of making a fresh start."

They go out into the light of three o'clock, the sun still very high because they are in the North. He gets into Élise's lilac-coloured car. He's very handsome, the last oblate. His cream-coloured shirt opens under a long black jacket and over a cross tattooed at his neck, the colour of the shadows under his tawny eyes. He had washed his hands in the holy water stoup, they taper, damp, onto powerful knees. Élise knows where to drive till nightfall.

He has never slept in a hotel. This one is a Hilton with sealed windows, in room 610 float the fumes of heating oil that pass through the walls overlooking a runway where airplanes touch down before the curfew. He sits upright in the high-backed easy chair; she forces him to begin again. On her knees, she loosens him and swallows him at the moment of the flayed final *A*, she is wearing the black jacket, the lace bodice won't be stained. He does not yet know how to touch her. Now he believes that he can learn and she believes that this angel won't kill her.

At dawn they wake and think they have repented. She tells him how he is to enter her, presently, after they have rubbed each other. She wants him on the carpet, which is stormy with the trails left by other men, other women, stale and faded from the truest passions. Full length, he positions himself and covers her. It happens inside, like eternal life. Warm rains that blend and whose odour they no longer notice.

At eight o'clock, at the Air Canada counter, they are betrothed. The flight that's about to leave is bound for New-foundland. It's foggy there, says the ticket lady, but they'll arrive by noon. They munch croissants, sip coffee, hold hands in the cabin; the hostess smiles only at them. They do not notice that the sky is still water and the travellers are wax.

Here is St. John's, faded soil, the shadow of the airport through the window. At Hertz all that's left is a grey car with dove-coloured upholstery and a radio that crackles the news of the day in English. A deep-sea fisherman has sacrificed his child in a pond, he bound her with seaweed. A prostitute has slashed her wrists on the steps of the House of Assembly and the guard satisfied himself before calling for help. The queen has called off her trip because an attendant killed the lieutenant-governor, who was caressing him. But the last oblate doesn't understand English and the Protestant churches along the winding road don't have confessionals.

They go. Towards Trouty, which is at the seaside on the map, the place where they will find a house forever. The houses must be blue, and pink, and mauve, perched miraculously on bare rocks beaten by a wuthering wind.

Élise says that she'll wash her yellow dress in rainwater, that she'll let it dry during clear spells, and that he will be able to take her at any time in her silk slip with the lace bodice, and that she will prepare cod with white wine imported from old countries whose language, still spoken here, she will learn. Sundays they'll spend at home or they'll cast bottles into the sea with messages of love that will come back to them with the tides, while the neighbour women speak ill of them and it gushes cold in the village at prayer.

Trouty is a town with the summer before it. The main street is a hill, the aluminum-sided houses are massed around the grocery store, the church is wood whose paint has worn away, its door is open onto faded rushes. That very evening they purchase the shack with its beautiful lanterns extinguished, the last house on the road out. Its front stoop seems to glide into the arm of the sound, the water that foams beneath a thickly veiled moon comes from as far away as the dancing rapid. At night they sleep in a narrow iron bed. They're hungry for milk and for strawberries, which are hard to find between their legs, for they too are cold. Tomorrow, they'll see to all that.

The cotton curtains turn pale and that's why it is six o'clock. Élise wants to touch the sea, which has withdrawn onto the mud where Trouty's debris dies, the shiny cans from the night before and the carcasses of yesterday's two-burner stoves. She turns around, her gaze empty, towards the man in black who is walking along the balustrade on the stoop, then she freezes. A fine rain falls onto their grey bodies. They will not touch each other until everything has been cleansed.

THE SON

"I'm forty years old and you aren't,"
sighed the woman seated at the table
(At that time the fruit of her womb
was deep inside another woman's belly)
He placed on the table a sex
that lay there, docile and white
as the neck of a dead bird
It was the end of their affair

When I was a child you were always losing me. The first time I remember — for there were others of which I know nothing save for that scratch on my forehead, inscribed there on the night when you expelled me from your womb, insisting on forceps — was at the cemetery. I had to pee. You were wailing into a big bouquet of white lilies, you whispered to me to go behind the granite column, over there beside the willow tree. My father was already in his grave, the earth was falling at the level of his navel, the sun was rising onto mine. When I came back the lilies formed a trail to where the limousine had been, it had disappeared with you in the back seat, and the young priest. Already he was promising you communion.

I was perfectly happy, you know, watching them fill the hole. I threw in some pebbles, the digger popped open a can of Pepsi that was nearly boiling, with him I drank the clotted blood of my father who would rather have died in the winter. The digger told me it was normal for a grieving woman to forget her child in the cemetery, some lose their minds as well, it could be that you didn't want to see me ever again. He had me chasing squirrels, then filling in another hole, a lot more cheerful because it was for a grand-mother who was rich, and there were fifteen of them who left behind roses and more roses.

At five o'clock he pointed, he settled me at his back on his motorbike, and I gave him the neighbours' address. They kept me there for a barbecue and their daughter poured me a few drops of wine. Her legs smelled of roses, too, it's entirely possible that I remember, it was such a beautiful day. Her name was Sylvia and when she took me home through the back door, she saw the beginning of the slap, which I dodged; she still talks about your criminal eyes, I always replied that they were the eyes of death because of my father, but probably I'm wrong because it's true that you didn't love him, and the very next day there was nothing left of him in the drawers or in the bathroom.

What was left was me, upstairs, at the end of the hallway, in the square bedroom you never set foot in. Sylvia also maintains that the blessed evening when the firemen came, when they flooded the square bedroom and I was able to sleep in my father's bed, it was you who started the fire. You didn't want to kill me, she said, you wanted to send me to a hospital for children where other widows would eventually take me as their son and call me Xavier, Vincent, Léon, Mathieu, depending on the day, there were so many places to fill inside their empty heads. My own name was Damien, do you remember that the room burned without me, that I was sleeping in the chaise longue next to the pool, that the noise of a siren wakened me? You never tried anything like that again, Sylvia suspected you. You forgot me at school, from one five o'clock to another, at the beach, at the movies, at Santa's Village, and on the slopes of Mount Orford. But by then I was thirteen and I wasn't lost any more.

I clung to your shadow, to the point of stealing it from you.

You were not as beautiful as you thought you were. It took me one hot summer, the harsh light on the patio and on your dips in the pool with your ingenue's cries, to work it out. I consigned you to a notebook, then to my computer, which you didn't even know how to turn on.

You have long toes, manicured all the way to the half-moons and painted a transparent ivory by Dior; but there's a bunion at the base of the big toe on your right foot, you hide it with wide-strapped sandals, you spend days locating them, in the spring, in shops where only saleswomen preside, you wouldn't want a man's eyes on the little bump that always spoils the shape of the leather, in the end. Your legs are slender and fairly well-shaped to the knee, they go well with your porcelain complexion; but some blue blood vessels show through there, one, on the left, in the fat of your calf, is twisted like the beginning of a varicose vein, it snakes and then fans out in pink threads, the capillaries make old ladies' patterns. You have spindle-shaped thighs, the kind that go on forever on the virgins in magazines, their flesh is hairless and it moves in fine waves even on the hardest chairs; but you have two stretchmarks at the edge of your groin, milky grooves, they dig into your belly, which I've never seen, under your bathing suit, but I know those grooves, they're mine, I think they run all the way up to your navel, taking the time to widen at the swelling in your abdomen I also left you, which you sometimes forget to pull in under a slightly protruding thorax. You have beautiful languid arms and the hands of a pianist, with fingers so long they tolerate nails that are barely rounded; but the middle finger is deformed like the toe, the knuckle knotted by housewife's arthritis. Your back is perfect, it flows straight from your shoulders to the small of your back without a mark, slate beige barely rippled by the line of the vertebrae that hold the nape of your neck so well; but under the left shoulder blade there's a brown spot, the shit mark that has grown along with you, the exact shape of a crab with one claw open, you can only see it in reverse, in a mirror, I assure you that when you see it the right way around you can tell that it's slimy, even scaly. I know about another, smaller one at the end of your long neck, at the base of the ear, which will shrivel and trickle at the first creases of old age, it won't be long. You have the Victorian face that suits untamed coils of hair, and matte cheeks, graphite eyes under heavy lids, a peaceful brow; but your lips have a rancid fold when you smile, one might say that they're closing, that they're holding onto what they seem to be giving, their corners will freeze if you continue like that. Your hair is fine and without colour, for the moment it curls slightly but it's the kind that falls out early, that leaves the lines of the skull uncovered.

I've also added up the beauty aids. The exfoliating and slenderizing creams by Clarins, the Dune body milk by Dior, the moisturizers for both day and night by Lancôme, the clay masque by Clinique, the firming capsules by Elizabeth Arden, the jellies for the delicate skin around the eyes by Estée Lauder, the Azulène mousse for the hair. Your colours are all by Lise Watier, they're made for our local brunettes, your perfume is also Dune, it's pervasive, I wonder if you're hiding the odour of the crab, with its traces of rotten seaweed and dread. When you're stripped of all that, when the chlorinated water of the pool evaporates after your brief afternoon swims, I smell it and I know.

For a long time I saw you entertain men at dusk, wearing yellow dresses that graze your ankles, delineate your hips, reveal your back but barely, that mingle with the glow of the lamps. You would pour them brightness along with the vodka, it would warm the first caresses, which always come from behind, which make the strap slip over the shoulder blade, then it was time to move on to your room, where I think you relaxed in the dark, for there was no shaft of light under the door. No men slept at your house, I heard nothing but the slamming of car doors around midnight. In the morning there wasn't even a droplet of strong sweat floating in the air, your sheets were in the laundry, you were fussing with the coffee.

Today, I don't know. I'm not there any more. Every evening I go to your friend's place, the blonde, short, round one who opens to me legs scraped clean with Ivory soap and who talks to me about you after I've been deep inside her, after I make her come with all your secrets. She said that you'd lost me for the pleasure of getting me back, that you've always hidden your breasts from me because I had drunk there and I had to forget your sour milk, that the night of the fire was a first wild desire, that men are appellants at dusk, that your door is open for me after midnight so that I can follow those men. It seems to me I've seen none of that in your eyes, which are still as they were at the cemetery. If you want to touch me, it's in order to lose me again.

I've mixed orange juice with the vodka you served me, that makes it yellow and yellow again with your July *pareo*, it bares your neck and the crab child. The weeping willow shivers and a shadow moves across the marble of the table, the temperature is thirty with a breeze from the northwest. In *Archives of Crime*, on the Internet, I read the story of a woman, ripe and ugly, who had adopted a crazy boy to marry when he turned eighteen, a priest blessed them, either to save them from hell or for a donation. They killed all the children they had, I printed up for you the drawing of the little crosses in their garden. It's just another story, you're much prettier than that monstrous woman, I am your son and I'm not lost.

You're sighing now, you say that you're forty years old and I'm not, that I don't understand anything. What do I have to do, Mama, with your smile that is shrinking again? I hold out to you my sex, docile and white, which your hand would not arouse. Don't tell me that it looks like the neck of a sleeping swan, I'll tell you that it's dying. Don't move, all I desire is some slight thing that's not you. And we shall never know what it was you wanted.

It's a magnificent day for moving to a new address.

THE ARABESQUE

She found love in a book
It was black and covered with ink
It left signs on her breasts
When the time came
she had trouble closing it

In musical dictations my score is always perfect. No one around me does as well. I can even distinguish a G sharp from an A flat at the beginning of a phrase, before I hear the rest, simply from the way that Florence Hébert presses on the black key, preoccupied on the sharp, lighter on the flat. Yet Florence's hands are always cold. She learned to play piano in the convent, a big wooden building on the shore of Lake Osisko where the frost seeped even into the stringed instruments. She claims to have been a boarder but it's possible she was a nun, it was at the end of that time. She wrote in pencil on the scores and only the sisters, it seems to me, would have used lead and eraser to make the sheets of music look like new, then unload them on beginners. Florence does so all the time with little girls sent by their mothers, long enough for them to stumble over the first eighth note, never to return. Florence's notebooks even have brown paper covers.

I've had mine for a long time, I order them from Archambault in Montreal, I don't cover them but keep them in a big filing drawer and never lend them to anyone, not even to Florence, who knows and never asks. She has nothing more to teach me anyway, my father pays her to get me into the conservatory. At home, scales get on his nerves but I still have to play them from eight to nine every day, for my shoulders. Shoulders are rotations, they guide arpeggios, every evening I rub them with petroleum-based liniment that makes my skin crack but feeds my bones, I can feel it. I don't tell anyone about that ointment, the other girls just have to get along with their arpeggios; anyway, Florence demands less of them. She lets them have the practice cubicles with a view of the other entrance to the conservatory, the one for the wind players who are mostly boys. I think it's vulgar to make sounds by blowing and besides, you have to play standing up most of the time and I'd rather sit down, my back straight, seeing nothing except the piano.

In my windowless cubicle there's a fairly high Gerhard Heintzman. It has better resonance than the Yamahas the conservatory's full of now because they don't cost as much. I hate anyone touching my Heintzman, I'm rarely away from it but I have to leave it sometimes, for the theory lessons I force myself to take every year, you never know what may have got away from one teacher or another. Last week I got a better understanding of accidental distortions in transposition, though I transpose perfectly. When I returned to my piano at eleven o'clock, I felt a sticky film under my fingers. I'm twenty-two years old, I know those teenage girls who stuff themselves with peanut butter in the morning and don't wash their hands properly. I take only non-fat cottage cheese on my toast and I scrub my hands with Le Chat soap from Marseille. My keys stay pure ivory and I never perspire.

I could have screamed but I never create scenes. I scrubbed it all away with an ammonia solution, then I rubbed the keys with a soft cloth. I've been working for ten days now on the *Arabesque*, opus 18, by Robert Schumann, I haven't even fully mastered the introductory motif. My method is very slow but it's the only one, measure by measure. The first one took me two days; beginnings always challenge me. *sol-si-la, sol-do. Leicht und zart*, says the Schirmer score. The thumb tends to accentuate the G on sixteenth notes, the fourth finger glides nicely onto the middle one for the *si-la*, but I add an unnecessary breath to the dotted eighth, then the second *sol* weighs down the clear *do* that the little finger should strike at the beginning of the second measure. It could be a whining lullaby.

Florence no longer gets involved but she listened to me yesterday, her presence modifies the echo, helps me to try it differently. She stayed till five p.m., that's when I put my books away. The corridor was empty and poorly waxed, as usual, she kept me on the stairs and talked to me again about going to Europe. She's been constantly urging me to go, ever since Marc-André Hamelin's tour, all Mozart and Chopin, with just a touch of Satie. I liked it. He played so clearly that I could name every note in every piece in my head, as if I were reading them. I told Florence that, she asked me what colour the pianist's hair was and whether I'd noticed the elegant grey cravat against his spotless shirt. She was tired, I think, her eyes were wild.

I did not reply. Not about Europe either, in fact, which I knew through music as well as I knew America. I have five recorded versions of the *Arabesque*, by Artur Rubinstein, Vladimir Horowitz, José Iturbi, Claudio Arrau, and Lucette Descaves. I like Lucette Descaves best because she doesn't get so carried away in the second movement and she doesn't drag out the final *molto tranquillo* where the others skitter about as if they've been caught in the rain. Lucette Descaves is the only one I'd like to meet if I were to go to Europe, but I can listen to her here just as well. I hear and I name every one of her notes, it doesn't matter to me if she's brunette or blonde, and if she had a shrill voice her comments would be unbearable. It took me years to get used to Florence's though it's just right, with neither low notes nor high.

All the same, she's been getting on my nerves lately, she has some ludicrous ideas.

About colour, for instance. She was walking home with me, as far as her usual turnoff near Lake Édouard, where there's a community project to plant flowers along the shore. We sat down for a moment, I rarely linger but she seemed so preoccupied. Had there not been a young woman in a grey wool dress who must have been sweating in the sun, everything would have been harmonious: the blue sky, the buttercups in flawless rows, a vast bed of cultivated orange hawkweed between the rocks. "Tomorrow," said Florence, "you may read about that woman jumping into the lake. The water is the same grey as her dress, she's come here to breathe the red, the gold, the blue that elude her, but her own colour is black. One can understand everything, even madness, through the shock of colours." The notes that I hear so clearly I'd grasp even better, she maintains, if I would stop naming them, if I were to show concern about what they say, like the colours of that woman who is going to commit suicide. I don't believe it. And I didn't read anything the next day, I never open a newspaper.

Two days later, I found a potted African violet on the filing cabinet in my cubicle. It was puny but blooming, still damp, I brushed its hairy leaves as I took it immediately to Florence, it was she who'd put it there, for my birthday. I explained to her that I'd received some records as gifts and that I was already quite annoyed because my father had chosen to give me all of Jacqueline du Pré's recordings, the cello is a perfectly viscous instrument. I claimed I was shutting myself away to listen to it but I merely undid the wrapping, there were some biographical notes on Jacqueline du Pré, she died very young. Florence wanted to tell me more about her life, but I had to go back to my scales, I thanked her for the violet, she'll look after it, I explained to her that the humidity or the odour could bother me.

I'm no longer calm, not really. There was also the morning when I discovered on the piano, where the score ought to be, a large reproduction of Renoir's *The Pianist*. I know people see the piano that way, a muddle of pink notes scattered before a young woman with brown braids, in the soft lamplight, in front of flowered tapestries, after dinner. But one plays perfectly only during the daytime, or at least in the daylight, one needs an empty stomach and better posture than that young woman, whose forearm isn't level. I gave the picture back to Florence, who claimed not to know where it came from.

And now there's the book. It showed up three days ago, it's entitled *Lettres d'amour, Robert et Clara Schumann*, published by Buchet Chastel in 1976. If I opened it, though it doesn't belong to me, it was because of the unsigned sepia drawing on the cover. Clara has my shoulders, round and firm, as well as the chignon that I tie as tight as hers, she, the nineteenth-century virtuoso whom I'll never hear play a note. I wanted to know how she had approached the *Arabesque*, written in 1838, during that correspondence. So I did my scales all the same, for one hour, and I didn't give the book back to Florence.

I've been reading slowly since this morning and now my stomach aches. There is nothing about the *Arabesque* in the letters from 1838 or after. There are just two beings who whine and moan and send each other kisses and who say atrocious things about music: *the sunbeam glittering on the grand piano and, what I particularly love, playing with the harmony of the sounds, after all it is only light set to music.* That's from Robert to Clara, that bilge. He offers her pearls shaped like tears, and an engagement ring, sometimes she nearly faints with happiness, sometimes the piano provides consolation for her tears.

I hate this book, I don't hear a single note in it, but I have trouble closing it. It's as if the two of them touch only by mail, but I see them when they finally meet again, they will have eight children, says the preface, it happened, he was constantly repeating, "it must happen." She certainly had to take off her dress and her stockings and he certainly had to lie naked on top of her and plunge into her while she said over and over, "my love, my everything," like in the letters. It is there, I now know, in the *Arabesque*, in the second movement, that powerful chord by the left hand that goes deeper while the right hand moans between F sharp and G, an octave too high. A line that I hear all at once, a groove that fills with lava, that snakes from thighs to belly, from belly to breasts, from breasts to shoulders. Mine. All the pages disgorge themselves into me, the ink rises to my eyes. I want to spit.

It is midnight. I am lying on the cold floor, but the intertwining continues, the hairy violet is growing in the small of my back, I have pink on my palms and the desire to be touched everywhere, with saliva and sweat. My name is Clara Wieck and it's been a hundred years since I died.

The young woman in the grey wool dress who jumped into Lake Édouard this morning was me. It took them twenty-four hours to find me, the time it took Florence to think about it. There are no signs of rape but there are scratches on my breasts, a small violence in the shape of a liana, you might have said an arabesque. The bottom of the lake is made up of sharp sediment, the medical examiner will confirm it.

Florence writes the eulogy. She says that I was going through that difficult period when one leaves romantic music behind to move on to the atonal, that I'd become enamoured of the shadowy side of a Schumann who died insane, that I heard voices under the notes, that I could no longer even pass a dictation. That I became infatuated with passing pianists, that I sought the open air and flowers, that I dreamed of going to Europe in search of passion. Art is a form of asceticism, she wrote in a chilly hand. Not everyone succeeds. Someone will make a retort about the monument to Robert and Clara Schumann on their grave in the Friedhof, in Bonn. Florence says I was moved by that supplicant at her husband's feet, watched over by cherubim. The scale will be reduced all the same. I died in a nowhere city and I was just a performer.

She killed me to get back the cubicle and the Gerhard Heintzman, or to prevent me from succeeding her with the little girls, I knew more about notes and theory than she did, I transposed perfectly, that sort of thing is known in a conservatory. She took back the book, she put it away, it is filled with trivia — *I am yours with all my heart and I kiss you lovingly and tenderly, for always.* She tells herself that I was a weakling to succumb to such paltry poison.

THE WITNESS

A finch falls from tree to pavement
A suicide
A girl in pink buries it under her bed
I know her
They had the same lover
Bare chest, tiny brain
it is he who kills virgins in America
between five and nine

The witness is an individual in his forties, a neighbour who, for three months, observed in minute detail the comings and goings of the suspect, whom the police think is violent and who is impossible to find. He could be hiding anywhere in America.

"I took my time before I said anything because I'm a cautious man," declared Monsieur Heller, a semi-retired insurance broker who had recently moved to the so pretty, so troubled village on the St. Lawrence. Now, though, he has plenty to say.

One of his policyholders died last year. He'd known him well, he was constantly reviewing his policy for the pleasure of visiting his perfect house, low and white and bright, where the widow wouldn't dare to live alone. She was wrong but he took advantage of her concerns to buy it, for a fair price; he wouldn't have exploited a client's wife. She really was wrong, the place was open to every beautiful thing, closed to all the horrors.

To the south, the house sits on loose stones that are sharp but slimy from the oil in the river, which give protection from intruders coming from the beaches and keep boats at a distance, though he can make out their occupants in the daytime. To the north, the huge property is divided into equal parts between a lawn that's prettily invaded by clover and a driveway where one could park ten cars, but there is only one, an aging grey Aries K, but he's not concerned because there is also, on the other side of the street, which is a little-used national highway, the corner store that takes care of his needs as far as newspapers, bottled water, pasta, and even the basic vegetables are concerned. To the east, under the kitchen windows, there extends all the way to the church the most flowery cemetery to be found in a cold country, three hundred years worth of dead whose descendants still live in the area, it will take him many seasons to decipher the families and their stories, a pastime common to talented insurance brokers. When necessary, he'll have the help of the priest whose presbytery stands next to the elegant charnel house. To the west, a tall house casts its shadow onto the front wall of his living room but he had cheerfully accepted this constraint, for in it lives the young teacher and principal of the last school in the village, still open with the Minister's permission. She would be an excellent neighbour and he would protect her when necessary, he'd thought as he was signing the deed.

He hoped to meet her as soon as he moved in, in April, but the opportunity didn't present itself, in fact it disappeared straight away. Last spring, you'll remember, was marked by an uncommon heat wave at a time when snow still lingers under the maples if not under the apple trees in our region. The temperature was at least thirty on the morning of Good Friday, when he saw pulling up at his neighbour's house a young man on a black motorbike, a rather ordinary machine, a Suzuki that struck him as being past its prime. The young man went inside for a few moments, then came back out with a trowel, a bucket, and various tools from the house. He started putting up a low wall between the adjoining driveways, a perfectly useless demarcation as the insurance man had no intention of encroaching on his neighbour's property, because she didn't have a car and he had all the room he needed for parking his.

The young man was working bare-chested. He was muscular, slim, already tanned, and he seemed fairly bright.

He had close-cropped hair, bluish black, he wore a ring in his left ear as is fashionable among young people nowadays, but his was enormous, three gold circles that brushed against his cheek when he was straining, one could see them from thirty metres away. Around noon the young woman appeared on the front stoop, with a blanket and a heavily laden tray. They shared some beer and what appeared to be a pizza under the big willow tree that lined the property on the school side. She must know him well, she was wearing a pink shirt that came just to her thighs over a pair of leggings, also pink. A schoolteacher doesn't dress that way for lunch with an ordinary worker. Their conversation was lively, they'd had two beers each, not one, she had gone inside to fetch them, and they'd smoked several cigarettes with the last one. Then he went back to work while she napped in a hammock slung across the deck in the back, where the river shuddered with false coolness. At six o'clock the boy had gone inside without knocking, put away the tools and pulled on his T-shirt, perhaps he'd showered because it had taken him a while and he seemed refreshed when he got back on the road.

It had taken him a week to finish the wall. The lunches under the willow had continued even after the Easter break; the school was next door. When winter returned for a few days, with freezing rain, work had gone on inside the house. He could spy a bit through his living-room window, not because he was trying to keep an eye on them but for reasons of conscience, the young woman could be in danger. Though the walls were made of stone, he thought he'd heard cries, which could certainly be those of coupling, but if the man was her lover, why did he always leave at five p.m.?

Villages aren't what they used to be. The corner store was run by a Vietnamese who had settled there with the help of a government program that was forcing immigration to regionalize; he wasn't talkative. Neither was the priest, to tell the truth. The old priest who lived in the presbytery had been, once, but he no longer went out, he contemplated what was left of his life from the back balcony, with a view of his grave and a few snow geese, already angels, that ate up his last temptations. The schoolchildren's parents were mostly from neighbouring parishes, they sent their progeny here in yellow buses and cared little about the life of a principal with whom they were satisfied; the children were fond of her, she always wore pink, she had a lovely smile, a decisive manner, and some knowledge of computers. The young man came and went during the daylight but only the neighbour bothered to observe him.

At the end of May, when the sun came back, he painted the mouldings of the house in an old blue that was all the rage for heritage properties. At noon they now covered their conversation with taped music made up of rumblings and electric howls that had the strange property of bringing out the birds. The young man hammered together a pink birdhouse with just one opening, which he hung rather high in the willow tree and a goldfinch moved in. Now they were certainly lovers.

There was ample proof, in fact. The neighbour had seen him standing by the hammock where the young woman was lying, her dress most likely unbuttoned to the hips so he could caress her, the movement of his arm was imperceptible but that's how women come most powerfully, under an infinitesimally gentle teasing of that tiny portion of their flesh. He had seen him inside on a day that was grey but bright, climbing up on a ladder, jeans tight on his ass but no doubt open in the front, where the young woman's curly head was resting, there's nothing better than an upright position for ejaculating into a mouth, for fully feeling her submission. He had seen him pretend to be repairing the flagstones on the patio but instead sniffing the pink leggings she'd put out on the railing to dry, that was the sign, he was sniffing cunt, the lout.

But he still left at five p.m., jumping onto his Suzuki, so noisy you could hear the clutch disengaging beyond the graveyard, where he turned onto the side road that leads to the highway. That's what had roused the insurance man, brought him out of the hypnotic state into which his observation had plunged him. The story was in the paper; only he knew how to read it. In the medium-sized city a hundred and twenty kilometres away, of which this village would one day be a suburb, there was a rapist at large who sometimes killed. It happened on hot nights when balcony doors stayed open. The survivors, all adolescent girls, talked about the sound of a motorbike; that was all they remembered, and that the man had close-cropped hair. His face was dark, his features blurred by their fear, there was nothing about an earring, a good way to put people off his scent. Undoubtedly, he took it off, he was a handyman who worked intelligently, though apparently — because of the earring — his intelligence wasn't overwhelming.

The investigator who had received the denunciation was smiling behind his fine eyeglasses, he was a bit of a sissy, he was the same age as the boys who wore earrings, he had listened politely to the insurance man but hadn't taken many notes. He should have, the justice system let the guilty man go free and now the young man is at large though the proof was clear, the trail fresh.

It was the first day of the school holidays, so beautiful they might have picnicked in the graveyard where the sun had risen like a caress, in the place where stillborn infants were buried. Then the sun had enveloped the whole village without touching it, the stones were as warm as the flowers, the river had woken up blue. Everything was ruined after the first coffee, of course, with the death rattle of the motorbike followed by that of a lawnmower, as if the boy couldn't wait for a more appropriate day to clean the small stretch of grass along the driveway, which disappeared at the road, which was in any case weakened by the dust. He was working bare-chested again, despite the weak sun. The goldfinch had appeared because of the noise and it stayed with them for the noon meal. The three of them talked together, whistling, warbling, speaking urgent words that sometimes seemed grave. It was then, from as far away as his own front stoop, where he sat reading the paper, that the neighbour clearly saw the bird light on the boy's shoulder, savouring some crumbs that were stuck to his sweaty neck; but it wasn't sweat, that long mauve weal running down his back, it was a groove that only a woman being raped would dig, all the way down to the small of his back. The sun was at its zenith, the light perfect, the wound brand-new. And the woman next door was in collusion. Before he went back to work, she had rubbed his back for a long time, her hand, coated with balm, followed the trace, penetrated there, sometimes seemed to get lost in the line of his buttocks. The boy had shuddered, straining like a cat, in fact that was how he looked at the bird, he knew how to attract quarry. Then he left at five p.m. and the next day, in the paper that arrived from the city at dawn, there was an account of how a teenage girl had been found dead in her isolated bedroom, her nails broken and her fingers covered with blood; the discovery had been made the night before, at the very moment when the guilty man was chatting about it under the willow with his two lovers.

To calm him, while suggesting that he not read so many novels, though he never read novels, the policeman had gone to the schoolteacher's house that same evening. She was quite astonished, the boy was her cousin and her childhood friend, he had a pretty girlfriend in town and he'd hurt himself helping her move, some sharp object had scraped him. That's what today's newspaper claims that she said, even though the boy never came back and there's no answer at the number she gave the police and virgins, suddenly, are no longer dying in the vicinity.

The sun comes up grey where they will bury the priest, around the middle of the summer. The goldfinch has lost his appetite, he began to chirp rather than sing, then he died as no bird before him has died. He perched high in the tree, on a branch bathed in light, he straightened up as if to take flight, he left the branch, his black-streaked wings held close to his thin body. His head struck the pavement, it was suicide. When she picked him up in one hand, she stroked the tiny round head for a long time, as if there were a brain inside that had been capable of loving. She went inside, she could have buried him under her bed. She doesn't go out any more.

Now the village comes alive. The distributor leaves twice as many copies of the tabloid newspaper, the parents are stirred all the same by a school principal who might have helped a murderer escape, they come to the corner store to get the news — business is booming — and they intend to place it on the agenda for the next school board meeting. A young reporter, summer help, determined to show his mettle, devotes his evenings to spying on the street. He's spent hours listening to the former insurance man, he passes on the man's theories, cautiously; his newspaper likes blood but fears libel suits. More daring, the host of a radio phone-in show has had the witness on three times, to inveigh with him against young men who sport earrings, who are either queers or murderers, in any case, perverts of one kind or another, and protected by charters.

Lured to the village, which he's seen on television, a major builder intends to build there a dozen townhouses in the New France style at affordable prices for the young families thanks to whom the school will never again be threatened with closing. In the meantime, the teacher has asked a local contractor to triple the height of the wall and to block her windows on the east side. Requests for permits in the village have multiplied, construction is flourishing, and everything else.

THE SCAFFOLD

Naked beneath her robe
she demanded the scaffold
for the handsome thief who stands there
"Her lips are honey
and my sting is innocent,"
he declared to the faltering judge
He impregnated her before the jury's eyes
The child was sentenced to life

Sixteen years ago I was teaching in the small town of X, one hundred and twenty kilometres from the village of Y, which I knew only by name, I'm rather sedentary and I prefer the mountains to the seashore that, through the river, ends up in this place, now peaceful but troubled at the time.

Because I had a reputation for sound judgement, like most history teachers, and particularly because I knew practically nothing about what had happened in Y and so could not have devised an opinion in advance, I was named a member of the jury by the two parties in a trial that looked as though it would be brief.

I didn't try to withdraw. The summer had been rather rainy after a strange heat wave in the spring. I had missed my annual trip to Provence because of a sprain I'd suffered when I slipped in the tub, a stupid accident from which I thought I was protected because I abstain from sports. I was feeling gloomy; the students who were arriving for their fifth year of secondary school seemed to me bigger ignoramuses than usual and, contrary to what people think, history cannot be taught to those who have no prior notion of the subject. Most of them didn't even know why they, in America, spoke French.

The distraction was welcome. It was a trial for a series of murders, a case rich in sensation, and I needed some in order to take up again with life, which I sensed slipping away from me a little more every year as I approached my thirties. I read a newspaper that doesn't cover trivia and the only stories I remembered had to do with my two fields of interest, *la question nationale* and union matters, vast historical muddles in such a small country where one mutation has been chasing away another for twenty years now. I was busy, I was writing and rewriting the outline for a book that I'd finally complete when I had the time that teaching doesn't allow. But I suspected that life also went on elsewhere; I had loved two women who had left me, one for an Italian and Italy, the other to smoke and drink as she pleased in comfort, activities I abstained from even while admitting that they must offer some pleasure with which I'd have to get acquainted.

In short, I was ripe for a break and the one the trial offered was ideal. I would have a ringside view of life without having to experience any drama myself, and through this temporary change of course, I was even going to enrich my understanding of history — the debate on capital punishment had resumed recently in the land, in the wake of the murder, by repeat offenders, of two young police officers, one of them a woman who had just completed her training. Normally such discussions don't interest me, history is far from repeating itself despite what people say, it's on the move and if barbarous cruelties do recur, those we relinquish are not repetitions of the originals. The last scaffolds disappeared from here when I was still playing hangman, my students didn't even know they'd once existed. I wanted to put myself to the test, however, the way we pinch ourselves to know if we're dreaming. I wanted to find out whether, in the face of the acts of violence attributed to the accused, the spirit of revenge, which is hidden under the desire to reestablish the order that existed before the horrors, was going to affect me.

Save for a locksmith who had seen all the vile acts of ordinary lives displayed behind the doors that he forced open, my fellow jurors struck me as a little too impressionable.

The women as much as the men, all middle-class and duly salaried, had appeared timid in the face of the lawyers' questions, stammering their personal information and, in my opinion, playing around with the truth a little when they declared they'd heard practically nothing about the case while I, who make a point of staying away from such disturbances of the common man, had no choice but to absorb the many rumours at the start of the new school year, when the presumed guilty man was apprehended. They, too, wanted to interrupt their everyday existences and, by selecting them, both the defense lawyer and the Crown prosecutor gave the signal that they wanted to play on sentiment. It was possible that I seemed malleable, my appearance is somewhat lackluster and my voice doesn't carry far.

The name of the accused was Maxime, like several others in his age group who were then entering their twenties. Though unremarkable, he was animated, one of those bright-eyed dark types who go through adolescence without mishap. He stood well, which is rare among us, shoulders back, neck shaved and straight, and while he wore a strange earring that could have irritated a jury, which when all's said and done was rather conservative, the rest of his attire, a very pale blue shirt with long sleeves and extremely well-cut grey trousers, inspired a certain confidence. He had, however, very strong hands that he did not try to conceal.

Four women had died and three had survived some extremely violent attacks — seven major offences — but the testimony lasted only a little more than a week. First came a parade of traditional regional policemen with thick moustaches and limited vocabularies, who displayed little evidence, lots of deductions, and even more prejudice with respect to a youth that was more idle along the St. Lawrence than elsewhere in the land. Maxime had no known address, his motorbike produced the noise that the survivors remembered; they also recognized his shaven neck, his killer's hands and his height, though they had a hard time distinguishing his face and, in their trauma, which continued before the court, it was impossible for them to gawk at the accused in any sustained fashion. We were awash in presumptions, which were highly disturbing but rather imprecise, the Crown even called as a witness a retired man who all summer had observed Maxime moonlighting at a neighbour's. The Crown prosecutor, a woman, tried to draw proof of his character from some odd behaviour. The defense summoned the neighbour to appear, a young school principal, pink and weary, who was his cousin, who loved him like a brother and who maintained he was a peaceable man, but nonetheless could not attest to his comings and goings after five p.m. every evening of the previous season.

We were in a state of lethargy when the accused finally testified. Until then, I had paid little attention to the representative of the Crown. She was a tiny bespectacled professional, the kind we see so many of now that the majority of students in our law faculties are women, and she made her way better than her opposite number through the order of the files. Impossible to guess at her body under the made-to-measure robe, but it must have been slender and silky to judge by her face with its full cheeks, its delicate nose, its olive complexion that was no doubt covered with the down that afflicts brunettes with thick hair; her own she wore pulled into one of those Victorian knots that bare the forehead too much and create a moon face. She must be a copy of her grandmother, whose dull existence in the shadow of some local notable she was avenging. Her name was actually Évangeline Dupré.

For five hours, she ruled over the premises. Without opposition, she strove to extirpate confessions that didn't come, but her intelligent questions, full of lugubrious innuendo, found a way to consider them as understood. In every minute of Maxime's time that was not accounted for, she placed a corpse, a torn vagina, lifeless eyes, and the beautiful names of the young women who'd had no choice. She brought back the night, the light sleep of the virgins, the silent commotion that swooped down on them, the mauve moment when it became pointless for them to refuse to die.

He resisted, denial after denial, his gaze was limpid, always. I felt rising in him, however, and in us, both surprise and fascination, as if she were telling a true story, as if she were the sole and irrefutable witness to so much pain. Their confrontation became violent under the fluorescent lighting in the windowless room, I would even say depraved, though I do not interpret that theatre in moral terms. Depraved because of what I saw with my own eyes, during the final exchange, when she spread her arms and leaned on the table that stood between them. The front of her robe fell open, she was naked, her flesh became the question. She was brutal. "You like sex?" He said yes with his eyes and with an imperceptible groan, which I saw him swallow. The defense objected and the judge, shaken though he had seen nothing, ordered an adjournment. I think I was the only one to have caught that bright flash of flesh from my angle of vision at the end of the front row. I confided in the locksmith, who'd become a close companion, who assured me that she was wearing a short beige dress, that it would have been inconceivable for her to be so bold as to make such an argument, risking her career, which was obviously off to a good start.

On the morning of her charge to the jury, I agreed that I'd been a victim of an illusion and prepared to get over it.

Évangeline Dupré's soliloquy was dazzling.

First she spoke to us, twelve uncertain men and women, potential weaklings. "Before your eyes, which have seen all there is to see on TV, grew dim, before your hearts were consoled without having experienced any cruelty, before your souls, forgiven in advance for all their despicable acts, there was in all of you," she reminded us, "a place for anger. It was planed down, destroyed, then it was forbidden you by the charlatans of this century's end — the priests, psychologists, social workers, community leaders, editorial writers, and philosophers who earn their livings and medals by defusing the bombs of your natural indignation, who subjugate you, you flock of sheep, so that you accept life as it is, with its well-managed turpitudes. The archangel who stepped on the head of the serpent, you look at today with amazement, as if he were a Nazi, the power of evil. And you no longer believe in the day of the Last Judgement because it is said to be a day of wrath, of a sin to be committed by God Himself, which is quite impossible when his pastoral imposes the soothing smile of forgiveness. Your brothers kill, they rape, and it's you who are guilty of seething and hating them, you make haste to dive into the warm water of reconciliation while your sisters are dying, you are their faded shrouds."

I felt a lump of rage rise, rage at her or at myself, when she turned to face the judge, an insipid soul nearing retirement, to show him where punishment lay. "You have been sitting there for thirty years because once your friends were in power," she told him, "but also because for hundreds of years, before Pontius Pilate became the idol of jurists fearful of any conclusion, buried under their footnotes, this place was a place for retribution. Lines of just men have overcome their mortal sorrow to stop evil and evildoers through fire, water, the stake, blade, rifle, poison. These have been — stripped bare, the face of Justice. Even today, when dictators are assassinated, entire democracies rejoice and celebrate the executioners. But this same day, thanks to your cowardice, they embrace those who kill their daughters. In this country, the most insignificant oiler of a scaffold was braver and wiser than the abolitionists, judges, and politicians who today no longer know how to cleanse their honour except on the golf course."

The judge bowed his head as if to the pillory; the prosecutor now addressed the accused. She recounted to him all his crimes, day after day of the summer lately flown, a serial that kept the courtroom under her spell for more than an hour. Then, holding Maxime's gaze, where flames were flaring, she explained to him, this time minute by minute, how she would have had his skin, how she'd have made him a hanged man had she not been surrounded by a shit-scared judge and jury, sheltered by the law. She described to him vertebrae cracking, viscera loosening, tongue disgorging, eyes rolling, lungs straining for one last gulp of air. And the horrible breeze that finally touches the brain, the ultimate farewell to earthly pleasures, which are the only genuine ones. Like those of the flesh. She described them to Maxime, exquisitely, how his muscular legs would have tightened around a woman's pelvis, how his young dog's tongue would have rasped all her lips, how he would have spilled again and again into a convulsed belly, and so on, during all the seasons that desire can wait. But instead, if there were such a thing as mercy for his victims, he must die an excruciating death.

She was standing against him, she was delivering her words to him in short gasps, rhythmical, inexhaustible. Some small thing refused to be consumed between them and we were all penetrated by that delirium, penetrated through our own genitals, until the condemned man set us free by taking her before our eyes. Yes, she was naked under the robe, and he impaled her, a few seconds of pure copulation before the officers woke up, came to, all hard no doubt, like me, who desired nothing but her.

"Her lips are honey and my sting is innocent," said her new lover. I could hear him clearly.

The affair caused a great stir, in the newspapers more than on television, as cameras were not admitted into the court. The judge declared a mistrial because of an error in drafting, the lawyer was stricken from the bar, the accused was later acquitted of the murders but not of the act of public indecency he had committed in the court of X. During his brief time in prison, he made himself into a poet. As for me, I was agitated for a long time, which was very good for me.

Yesterday I learned that a child had been born of that act. He is fifteen years old now, he's registered in one of my classes, he was raised in foster families, Évangeline Dupré hadn't wanted any son of her hanged man. The boy knows. He asked me to relate his life sentence to him. And so that was the story, which will have no end.